The
French Classical Romances

Complete in Twenty Crown Octavo Volumes

Editor-in-Chief

EDMUND GOSSE, LL.D.

With Critical Introductions and Interpretative Essays by

HENRY JAMES PROF. RICHARD BURTON HENRY HARLAND

ANDREW LANG PROF. F. C. DE SUMICHRAST

THE EARL OF CREWE HIS EXCELLENCY M. CAMBON

PROF. WM. P. TRENT ARTHUR SYMONS MAURICE HEWLETT

DR. JAMES FITZMAURICE-KELLY RICHARD MANSFIELD

BOOTH TARKINGTON DR. RICHARD GARNETT

PROF. WILLIAM M. SLOANE JOHN OLIVER HOBBES

Octave Feuillet

OCTAVE FEUILLET

The Romance of a Poor Young Man

TRANSLATED FROM THE FRENCH
BY C. G. COMPTON

WITH A CRITICAL INTRODUCTION
BY HENRY HARLAND

A FRONTISPIECE AND NUMEROUS OTHER PORTRAITS WITH DESCRIPTIVE NOTES BY OCTAVE UZANNE

P. F. COLLIER & SON
NEW YORK

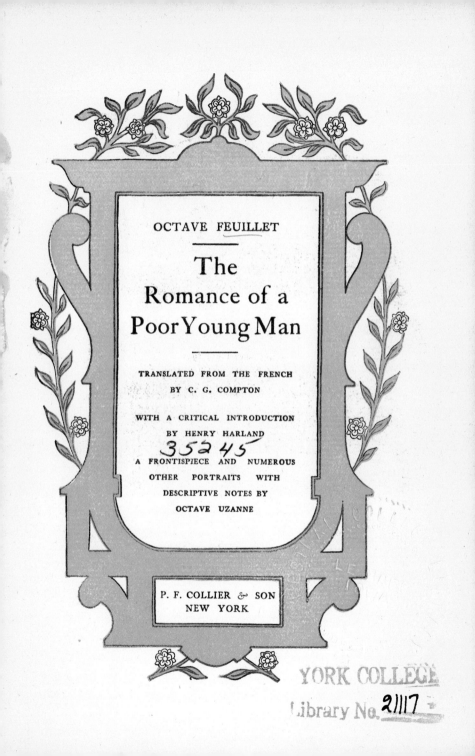

OCTAVE FEUILLET'S NOVELS

To be serious seriously is the way of mediocrity. To be serious gaily is not such an easy matter. To look on at the pantomime of things, and to see, neatly separated, tragedy here, comedy opposite—to miss the perpetual dissolution and resolution of the one into and out of the other—is inevitable when eyes are purblind. *Diis aliter visum.* Olympus laughs because it perceives so many capital reasons for pulling a long face; and half the time pulls a long face simply to keep from laughing. I imagine it is in some measure the Olympian manner of seeing which explains the gay seriousness of the work of Octave Feuillet.

Octave Feuillet possesses to an altogether remarkable degree the art of being serious not only gaily, but charmingly. This, to begin with, places him and his stories in a particular atmosphere; and, if we consider it, I think we shall recognise that atmosphere as something very like the old familiar atmosphere of the fairy-tale. At any rate, there is a delicate, a fanciful symbolism in Feuillet's work, which breathes a fragrance unmistakably reminiscent of the enchanted forest. For an instance, one may recall the chapter in *Un Mariage dans le Monde* which relates the escapade of Lionel and his betrothed on the day before their wedding. A conventional mother, busy with preparations for the ceremony, intrusts her daughter to the chaperonage of an old aunt, who is, we might suppose, exactly the person for the office. But old aunts are sometimes wonderfully made; sometimes they keep the most unlooked-for surprises up those capacious old-fashioned sleeves of theirs. This one was a fairy godmother in disguise, and, I suspect, a pupil of the grimly-benevolent Blackstick. With good-humoured cynicism, she remarks that the happiest period of even the happiest married life is the day before it begins, and she advises her young charges to make the most of it—chases them, indeed, from her presence. "Be off with you, my children! Come, be off with you at once!" They escape to the park, where they romp like a pair of truant school-children. That is all; but in Feuillet's hands it becomes a fairy idyl. It serves, besides, the symbolic purpose of striking at the outset the note of joyousness which he means to repeat at the end, though the book is one that threatens, almost to the last page, to end on a note of despair. For *Un Mariage dans le Monde*, if far from being the most successful of Feuillet's novels, exhibits, none the less, some of his cleverest craftsmanship. He hoodwinks us into the fear that he meditates disaster, only pleasantly, genially, at the right moment, to disappoint us with the denouement we could have wished.

Feuillet's geniality, for that matter, runs through all his books, and is one of the vital principles of his talent. It is never the flaccid geniality, the amiability, of the undiscerning person; it is, rather, the wise and alert geniality of the benign magician, who is sometimes constrained to weave black spells, because that is a part of the game, and in the day's work, as it were, but who puts his heart only into the weaving of spells that are rose-coloured. This is perhaps why Feuillet's nice people nearly always take flesh and live and breathe, his horrid people hardly ever—another resemblance, by-the-bye, between him and the writer of fairy-tales. The nice women, with their high-bred lovers, who step so daintily through his pages, to the flutter of perfumed fans and the rustle of fine silks, are as convincing as the palpitantly convincing princesses of Hans Andersen and Grimm; but Feuillet's villains and adventuresses, like the ogres and the witches we never very heartily believe in, are, for the most part, the merest stereotypes of vice and wickedness, always artificial, too often a trifle absurd.

In *Monsieur de Camors*, for example, we have an elaborate study of a man who has determined to live by the succinct principle, "Evil, be thou my good" —a succinct enough principle, in all conscience, though Feuillet requires a lengthy chapter and a suicide to enunciate it. The idea, if not original, might, in some hands, lend itself to interesting development; but not so in Feuillet's. From the threshold we feel that he is handicapped by his theme. It hangs round his neck like the mill-stone of the adage; it checks his artistic impulses, obscures his artistic instincts. The quips and cranks, the wreathed smiles, of Feuillet the humourist, were out of place in a stupendous epopee of this sort; so, for the sake of a psychological abstraction, which hasn't even the poor merit of novelty, we must look on ruefully, while our merryman, divested of cap and bells, proses to the end of his four sad hundred pages. There are novelists who must work with an abstraction, who can see their characters and their incidents only as they illustrate an abstraction; and these also achieve their effects and earn their rewards. But Feuillet belongs in a different galley. A handful of human nature, a pleasing countryside, and Paris in the distance—these are his materials. The philosophy and the plot may come as they will, and it really doesn't much matter if they never come at all. To give Feuillet a subject is to attach a chain and ball to his pen. He is never so debonair, so sympathetic, so satisfying a writer, as when he has something just short of nothing to write about.

In *Monsieur de Camors* he has a tremendous deal to write about; his subject weighs his pen to the earth. The result is a book that's a monstrosity, and a protagonist who's a monster. Louis de Camors is as truly a monster as any green dragon that ever spat fire or stole king's daughters (though by no means so exciting a monster), and he hasn't even the virtue of being a monster that hangs together. For, while we are asked to think of him as destitute of natural affections, he is at the same time shown to us as the fond idolater of his wife, his wife's mother, and his son. On his son's account, indeed, he goes so far as to spend a long cold night in a damp and uncomfortable wood, only to be dismissed in the morning without the embrace, in the hope of gaining which he has violated his philosophy and taken the chances of rheumatism. Altogether a man devoid of affections, who loves his son, his wife, and his mother-in-law, may be regarded as doing pretty well. Again (since we are on the chapter of inconsistencies), in that dreary and pompous letter written to Louis by his father, which expounds the text of what becomes the son's rule of conduct, he is gravely charged to fling religion and morality out of the window, but to cherish "honour" as it were his life. "It is clear that a materialist can't be a saint, but he can be a gentleman, and that is something," complacently writes the elder Comte de Camors. Louis, however, though he makes loud acts of faith in this inexpensive gospel, never hesitates to betray his friend, to seduce the wife of his benefactor, nor to marry an unsuspecting child, who loves him, for the sheer purpose of screening an intrigue with "another lady," which he still intends to carry on. Feuillet, perhaps, saves his face by heaping upon this impossible being's head all the punishments that are poetically due to crime, but he doesn't save *Monsieur de Camors*. It is a dismal volume, uncommonly hard to read. And yet —art will out; and dismal as it is, it presents to us one of Feuillet's most captivating women, Louis de Camors' ingenuous little wife. Listen to her artless pronouncement upon Monsieur's evangel of "honour." "Mon Dieu," she says, "I'm not sure, but it seems to me that honour apart from morality is nothing very great, and that morality apart from religion is nothing at all. It's like a chain: honour hangs in the last link, like a flower; but when the chain is broken, the flower falls with the rest."

If, however, Feuillet's villains are failures, his adventuresses and bad women are grotesquer failures still. And no wonder. His reluctance to fashion an ugly thing out of material that would, in the natural course of his impressions, suggest to him none but ideas of beauty, is quite enough to account for it. Octave Feuillet is too much a gentleman, too much a *preux chevalier*, to be able to get any intellectual understanding of a bad woman; the actual operations of a bad woman's soul are things he can get no "realizing sense" of. So he dresses up a marionette, which shall do all the wicked feminine things his game necessitates, which shall plot and poison, wreck the innocent heroine's happiness, attitudinize as a fiend in woman's clothing, and even, at a pinch, die a violent death, but which shall never let us forget that it is stuffed with saw-dust and moved by strings. Madame de Campvallon, Sabine Tallevaut, Mademoiselle Hélouin, even Julia de Trécœur—the more they change, the more they are the same:

sister-puppets, dolls carved from a common parent-block, to be dragged through their appointed careers of improbable naughtiness. You can recognise them at once by their haunting likeness to the proud beauties of the hair-dresser's window. They are always statuesque, always cold, reserved, mysterious, serpentlike, goddesslike—everything, in fine, that bad women of flesh and blood are not. Octave Feuillet, the wit and the man of the world, knows this as well as we do; and knowing it, he tries, by verbal fire-works, to make us forget it. "She charms me—she reminds me of a sorceress," says some one of Sabine Tallevant. "Do you notice, she walks without a sound? Her feet scarcely touch the earth—she walks like a somnambulist—like Lady Macbeth." It is the old trick, the traditional *boniment* of the showman; but not all the *boniments* in Feuillet's sack can make us believe in Sabine Tallevaut.

One can recognise Feuillet's bad women, too, by the uncanny influence they immediately cast upon his men. "More taciturn than ever, absent, strange, as if she were meditating some profound design, all at once she seemed to wake; she lifted her long lashes, let her blue eyes wander here and there, and suddenly looked straight at Camors, who was conscious of a thrill"—that is how Mme. de Campvallon does it, and the fact is conclusive, so far as her moral character is in question. None of Feuillet's good women would ever dream of making a man "thrill" at her first encounter with him. But Feuillet's bad women will stop at nothing. Julia de Trécœur takes her own step-father, a middle-aged, plain, stout, prosaic country gentleman, and throws him into a paroxysm that has to be expressed in this wise: "It was a mad intoxication, which the savour of guilt only intensified. Duty, loyalty, honour, whatsoever presented itself as an obstacle to his passion, did but exasperate its fury. The pagan Venus had bitten him in the heart, and injected her poisons. A vision of Julia's fatal beauty was present without surcease, in his burning brain, before his troubled eyes. Avidly, in spite of himself, he drank in her languors, her perfumes, her breath."

Julia de Trécœur has sometimes been called Feuillet's master-piece. One eminent critic remarks that in writing it Feuillet "dived into the vast ocean of human nature, and brought up a pearl." Well, there are pearls and pearls; there are real pearls and artificial pearls; there are white pearls and black pearls. It might seem to some of us that *Julia de Trécœur* is an artificial black one. Frankly, as a piece of literature, the novel is just in three words a fairly good melodrama. Julia herself is the proper melodramatic heroine. Her beauty is "fatal," her passions are ungovernable, and she dearly loves a scene. Now she contemplates retirement into a convent, now matrimony, now a leap from the cliffs; and each change of mood is inevitably the occasion for much ranting and much attitudinizing. Her history is a fairly good melodrama. That it is not a tip-top melodrama is due to the circumstance that Feuillet was too intelligent a man to be able to make it so. He can't keep out his wit; and every now and again his melodrama forgets itself, and becomes sane comedy. He can't keep out his touches of things simple and human; the high-flown, unhuman remainder suffers from the contrast.

Why, one wonders, with his flair for the subtleties of the normal, with his genius for extracting their charm from trifles, why should Feuillet have turned his hand to melodrama at all? Is it partly because he lived in and wrote for a highly melodramatic period—"the dear, good days of the dear, bad Second Empire"? Partly, too, no doubt, because, as some one has said, the artist can never forgive, though he can easily forget, his limitations. Like the comic actor who will not be happy till he has appeared as Hamlet, the novelist, also, will cherish his unreasoning aspirations. And then, melodrama is achieved before you know it. Any incident that is not in itself essentially *un*dramatic will become melodramatic, when you try to treat it, it will become forced and stagey, if dramatic incidents are not the spontaneous issue of your talent. Dramatic incidents are far from being the spontaneous issue of Feuillet's talent; they are its changelings. His talent is all preoccupied in fathering children of a quite opposite complexion. Style, suavity, elegance, sentiment, colour, atmosphere—these are Feuillet's preoccupations. Action, incident, are, when necessary, necessary evils. So his action, when he is at his best, loiters, saunters, or even stops dead-still; until suddenly he remembers that, after all, his story must some time reach its period, and that something really must happen to advance it. Thereupon, hurriedly, perfunctorily, carelessly, he "knocks off" a few pages of incident—of incident fast and furious—which will, as likely as not, read like the prompt-book of a play at the Adelphi.

That absurd Sabine Tallevaut, whose feet scarcely touch the earth, with poison in her hand and adultery in her heart, is the one disfigurement upon what might otherwise have been Feuillet's most nearly perfect picture. In spite of her, *La Morte* remains a work of exquisite and tender beauty; and I'm not sure whether Aliette de Vaudricourt isn't the very queen of all his women. If Feuillet was too much a gentleman to be able to paint a bad woman, he was too much a man not to revel in painting a charming one. As we pass through his gallery of delightful heroines, from Aliette de Vaudricourt to Clothilde de Lucan, to Mme. de Técle, Marie FitzGerald, "Miss Mary" de Camors, Marguerite Laroque, even to Jeanne de Maurescamp, we can feel the man's admiration pulsing in every stroke of the artist's brush. He takes the woman's point of view, espouses her side of the quarrel, offers himself as her champion wherever he finds that a champion is needed. And he sticks to his allegiance even after, as in the case of Jeanne de Maurescamp, she might seem to have forfeited her claim to it. Of Jeanne he can still bring himself to say, at the end of *L'Histoire d'une Parisienne*: "Decidedly, this angel had become a monster; but the lesson of her too-true story is, that, in the moral order, no one is born a monster. God makes no monsters. It is man who makes them."

In this instance, however, Feuillet is, perhaps,

rather the apologist than the champion. His contention is that Jeanne was by nature virtuous, and that her virtue has been destroyed by the stupidity and the brutality of her ill-chosen husband. But Feuillet has too fine and too judicious a wit to insist upon the note of strenuousness. Seeing the woman's point of view, he sees its humours as well as its pathos. Admitting that men for the most part are grossly unworthy of her, and that woman has infinitely the worst of it in the arrangements of society, admitting and deploring it, he doesn't profess to know how to set it right; he has no practical reform to preach. His business is to divert us, and, if he must be serious, to be serious gaily and charmingly. And perhaps he is most serious, not when composing an epitaph for Jeanne de Maurescamp, but when he is lightly saying (in the person of the Comtesse Jules): "Always remember, my poor dear, that women are born to suffer—and men to be suffered."

Charmingly serious himself, Feuillet's heroines likewise are always serious, in their different charming ways. They may be wilful and capricious, like Marguerite Laroque, or fond of the excitements of the world, like Mme. de Rias, or wise in their generation, like Mme. de la

Veyle, but they are always womanly and human at the red-ripe of the heart, and they are almost always religious. A sceptic, scepticlike, Feuillet utterly discountenances scepticism in woman. Even his most recusant of masculine unbelievers, the Vicomte de Vaudricourt, proclaims his preference for a pious wife. "Not, of course," he says, "that I exaggerate the moral guarantees offered by piety, or that I mistake it for a synonym of virtue. But still it is certain that with women the idea of duty is rarely dissociated from religious ideas. Because religion doesn't keep all of them straight, it is an error to conclude that it keeps none of them straight; and it's always well to be on the safe side." Elsewhere Feuillet gives us his notion of the moral outlook of the woman who is not religious. Evil for her, he tells us, ceases to be evil, and becomes simply *inconvenance.* 'Tis a very mannish, a very Frenchmannish, way of viewing the thing.

One has sometimes heard it maintained that only women can reveal themselves with perfect grace in a form so intimate as letters or a diary; that a man's hand is apt to be too heavy, his manner too self-conscious. Perhaps it is Feuillet's sympathy with women that has made him the dab he is at this womanly art. In *La Morte*, for instance, we learn vastly more of Bernard's character from his diary than we should from thrice the number of pages of third-personal exposition. The letters from Marie to her mother, in *Monsieur de Camors*, furnish the single element of relief in that lugubrious composition. Even those that pass between Rias and Mme. de Lorris, in *Un Mariage dans le Monde*—though their subject-matter is sufficiently depressing, though the man is an egotistical cad, and the great lady who is giving him her help and pity ought rather to despise and spurn him—are exceedingly good and natural letters; and the letter from Mme. de Rias to Kévern, which ends the book, is a very jewel of a letter. But it is in the diary of his poor young man that Feuillet's command of the first person singular attains its most completely satisfying results.

Le Roman d'un Jeune Homme Pauvre is a tale of youth, for the young; and the eldest of us may count himself still young if he can still enjoy it. Here we have romance pure and simple, a thing of glamour all compact; and the danger-line that so definitely separates romance from absurdity, yet leaves them so perilously near together, is never crossed. The action passes in the country, and in the most delectable sort of country at that—the country of the appreciative and imaginative cit. Before all things a Parisian, Feuillet is never particularly happy in presenting Paris. His Paris is correct enough in architecture and topography, no doubt; but the spirit of Paris, the whatever it is which makes Paris Paris, and not merely a large town, somehow evades him. Possibly he knew his Paris too well; familiarity had bred a kind of inability to see, to focus, a kind of "staleness." Anyhow, it is when he gets away from Paris that he wakes to the opportuneness and the opportunities of scenic backgrounds. His eye, "stale" to town, is now all eagerness, all freshness. Impressions of beauty crowd upon him. He sees the country as it is doubtful whether the countryman ever sees it—the countryman who has been surfeited with it, who has long since forgotten its first magical effect. He brings to the country the sensitiveness which is the product of the city's heat and strife. Dew and wild flowers, the green of grass and trees, the music of birds, the flutter of their wings, the pure air, the wide prospects, the changing lights—it is to the appreciative and imaginative townsman that these speak their finest message.

But Feuillet is more than a townsman: he is a teller of fairy-tales. To him the country is a free playground for his fancy. There beautiful ladies and gallant knights have nothing to do but to love and to sing; and there, without destroying our illusion, he can leave them to live happily forever after. The Brittany, in which Maxime and Marguerite meet and misunderstand and woo and wed, is not that northwestern corner of France that one can reach in a few hours by steamer from Southampton; it is a Brittany of fairy woods and streams and castles, that never was, save in the poet's dream. For if others of Feuillet's novels have been only in part fairy-tales, or only rather like fairy-tales, the *Romance of a Poor Young Man* is a fairy-tale wholly and absolutely. The personages of the story are the invariable personages of the fairy-tale: the prince disguised as a wood-cutter, in the Marquis de Champcey disguised as a farm-bailiff; the haughty princess, who will not love, yet loves despite her will, and is rewarded by the wood-cutter's appearing in all the prince's splendour at the proper time, in Marguerite Laroque; the bad prince and the bad princess, in M. de Bévallon and Mlle. Hélouin; the good magician, in M. Laubépin; and the delightfullest of conceivable fairy godmothers, in Mlle. de Porhoët. And the progress of the story is the wonted progress of the fairy-tale. There is hardship, but it is overcome; there are perils, but they are turned; misconceptions, but they are cleared up. There are empty pockets, but there is the bag of gold waiting to fill them. The marvellous never shocks our credulity, the longest-armed coincidences seem the most natural happenings in the world. We are not in the least surprised when, at the right moment, the bag of gold appears at Maxime's feet, enabling him to marry; it is the foregone consequence of his having a fairy godmother. We don't even raise the eyebrow of doubt when the Laroques contemplate relinquishing their fortune to the poor, so that Marguerite may come to her lover empty-handed; that is the accepted device of the fairy-tale for administering to the proud princess her well-deserved humiliation. In one small detail only does the fairy-tale teller lose himself, and let the novelist supplant him; that is where he implies that the bad prince and princess, after their wicked wiles had been discovered, took the train to Paris. They did nothing of the sort. They were turned into blocks of stone, and condemned to look on at the happiness of the good prince and princess from the terrace of the Château de Laroque.

But it must not be supposed, because the personages of the *Romance of a Poor Young Man* are fairy-tale personages, that therefore they are not human personages. It is, on the contrary, the humanity of its personages that makes your fairy-tale interesting. You stick to human men and women, you merely more or less improve the conditions of their existence, you merely revise and amend a little the laws of the external universe—an easy thing to do, in spite of the unthinking people who prate of those laws as immutable. Then the fun consists in seeing how human nature will persist and react. Surely none of Feuillet's heroines is more engagingly human than Marguerite Laroque. It is true that we see her only through the eyes of a chronicler who happens to be infatuated with her, but we know what discount to allow for that. We are confident from her first entrance that if, as we hope, our poor young man's head is screwed on as poor young men's heads should be, Marguerite will turn it. We learn that she is capricious, therefore Maxime will be constant; that she is proud, therefore, in all humility, he will be prouder; that she is humble, therefore, in all pride, he will humble himself at her feet. But antecedent to all this, and just because his ostensible business in Brittany is the management of the Laroques' estate, no one needs to warn us that his real business will be the conquest of the Laroques' daughter. We can foresee with half an eye that the affairs of the estate are affairs which our disguised marquis will conscientiously neglect. Indeed, Mme. Laroque herself seems to have been haunted by something of the same premonition. What does she say to the sous-préfet? "Mon Dieu, ne m'en parlez pas; il-y-a là un mystère inconcevable. Nous pensons que c'est quelque prince déguisé. . . . Entre nous, mon cher sous-préfet, je crois bien que c'est un très-mauvais intendant, mais vraiment c'est un homme très-agréable."

She might have added "un homme très-digne." For if we have a fault to find with Maxime, it is that he seems just possibly a thought too "digne." But that is a fault common to so many men in fiction. French novelists, like English lady novelists, are terribly apt to make their men too "digne" —when they don't make them too unspeakably *indigne*. Maxime, however, we mustn't forget, is his own portraitist, and we'll hope in this detail the portrait errs. For the rest, we are content to accept it as he paints it. He is a poor young man, but he is also a fairy prince. Therefore he can vaunt himself as an ordinary poor young man could hardly do with taste. He can perform and narrate his prodigies of skill and valour without offending. He can rescue an enormous Newfoundland dog from a raging torrent, for example, with the greatest ease in the world, an exploit you or I might have found ticklish, and he can tell us of it afterward, a proceeding you or I might have shrunk from as vainglorious. For Maxime is a fairy prince; the dog belongs to the fairy princess; and the bad prince, the rival, who is standing by, doesn't know how to swim. Again, with splendid indifference, he can accomplish and record his leap from the Tour d' Elven to save the fairy princess from a situation that might, in Fairyland, have compromised her; hadn't the princess unjustly impugned his honour, and insinuated that the situation was one he had deliberately brought to pass? "Monsieur le Marquis de Champcey, y a-t-il eu beaucoup de lâches dans votre famille avant vous?" superbly demands Marguerite; and we can see her kindling eye, the scornful curl of her lip, we can hear the disdainful tremor of her voice. Maxime would be a poor-spirited poor young man, indeed, if, after that, he should hesitate to jump. And he has his immediate compensation. "Maxime! Maxime!" cries the haughty princess, now all remorse, "par grâce, par pitié! au nom du bon Dieu, parlez-moi! pardonnez-moi!" So that, though the prince goes away with a broken arm, the lover carries exultancy in his heart.

Is Maxime perhaps just a thought too "digne,"

also, in his relations with his little sister—when he visits her at school, for instance, and promises to convey the bread she cannot eat to some deserving beggar? At the moment he is the most deserving beggar he chances to know of, but he is resolved to keep his beggary a secret from Hélène. "Cher Maxime," says she, "à bientôt, n'est-ce pas? Tu me diras si tu as rencontré un pauvre, si tu lui as donné mon pain, et s'il l'a trouvé bon." And Maxime, in his journal: "Oui, Hélène, j'ai rencontré un pauvre, et je lui ai donné ton pain, qu'il a emporté comme une proie dans sa mansarde solitaire, et il l'a trouvé bon; mais c'était un pauvre sans courage, car il a pleuré en devorant l'aumône de tes petites mains bien-aimées. Je te dirai tout celà, Hélène, car il est bon que tu saches qu'il y a sur la terre des souffrances plus sérieuses que tes souffrances d'enfant: je te dirai tout, excepté le nom du pauvre." It certainly *is* "digne," isn't it? Is it a trifle too much so? Isn't it a trifle priggish, a trifle preachy? Is it within the limits of pure pathos? Or does it just cross the line? I don't know.

I am rather inclined to think that Maxime is at his best—at once most human and most fairy princelike—in his relations with the pre-eminently human fairy Porhoët. He is entirely human, and weak, and nice, when he blurts out to her the secret of his high birth. Hadn't she just been boasting of her own, and invidiously citing Monsieur l'intendant as a typical plebeian? "En ce qui me concerne, mademoiselle," he has the human weakness to retort, "vous vous trompez, car ma famille a eu l'honneur d'être alliée à la vôtre, et réciproquement." He remains human and weak throughout the somewhat embarrassing explanations that are bound to follow; and if, in their subsequent proceedings, after she has adopted him as "mon cousin," he will still from time to time become a trifle priggish and a trifle preachy, we must remember that mortal man, in the hands of a French novelist, has to choose between that and a career of profligacy.

It is by his *Roman d'un Jeune Homme Pauvre* that Feuillet is most widely known outside of France; it is by this book that he will "live," if he is to live. Certainly it is his freshest, his sincerest, his most consistently agreeable book.

HENRY HARLAND.

BIOGRAPHICAL NOTE

OCTAVE FEUILLET *was born at Saint-Lô, in the department of the Manche, on the 11th of August, 1821. His father, who belonged to one of the oldest Norman families, was secretary-general to the prefect, and a little later, in the revolution of 1830, played a prominent part in politics. A hereditary nervousness, amounting finally to a disease, alone prevented him, according to Guizot, from being given a portfolio in the new ministry. Octave inherited his father's excessive sensibility, although in later years he held it more under control. After the death of his mother, which occurred as he was developing in boyhood, he became so melancholy that, at the advice of the physicians, he was sent to a school in Paris, where his health gradually became re-established; afterward, at the Collège de Louis-le-Grand, he greatly distinguished himself as a scholar. It was his father's design to prepare him for the diplomatic career, but already the desire to write had awakened itself in him. When the moment came for choosing a profession, Octave timidly confessed his determination to make literature his business in life; the irascible old gentleman at Saint-Lô turned him out of the house, and cut off his allowance. He returned to Paris, and for three years had a hard struggle with poverty. During this time, under the encouragement of the great actor Bocage, Octave Feuillet brought out three dramas, "Échec et Mat," "Palma," and "La Vieillesse de Richelieu," under the pseudonym of "Désiré Hazard." These were successful, and the playwright's father forgave and welcomed him back to his favour. Octave remained in Paris, actively engaged in literary work, mainly dramatic, but gradually in the line of prose fiction also. In 1846 he published his novel of "Polichinelle," followed in 1848 by "Onesta," in 1849 by "Rédemption," and in 1850 by "Bellah." None of these are remembered among Octave Feuillet's best works, but he was gaining skill and care in composition. In 1850, however, he was suddenly summoned home to Saint-Lô by the increased melancholy of his father, who could no longer safely be left alone in the gloomy ancestral mansion which he refused to leave. Octave, with resignation, determined to sacrifice his life to the care of his father, and in this piety he was supported by his charming cousin, Valérie Feuillet, a very accomplished and devoted woman, whom he married in 1851. For eight years they shared this painful exile, the father of Octave scarcely permitting them to leave his sight, and refusing every other species of society. Strangely enough, this imprisonment was not unfavourable to the novelist's genius; the books he wrote during this period—"Dalila," "La Petite Comtesse" (1856), "Le Village," and finally "Le Roman d'un Jeune Homme Pauvre (1858)—being not only far superior to what he had previously published, but among the very finest of all his works. By a grim coincidence, on almost the only occasion on which Octave Feuillet ventured to absent himself for a day or two, to be present at the performance of his "Roman d'un Jeune Homme Pauvre," when it was dramatized in 1858, the father suddenly died while the son was in Paris. This was a great shock to Feuillet, who bitterly and unjustly condemned himself. He was now, however, free, and, with his wife and children, he returned to Paris. He was now very successful, and soon became a figure at Compiègne and in the great world. In 1862 he published "Sibylle," and was elected a member of the French Academy. A great favourite of the Emperor and Empress, he was tempted to combine the social life at Court with the labours of literature. His health began to suffer from the strain, and, to recover, he retired again to Saint-Lô, where he lived, not in the home of his ancestors, but in a little house above the ramparts, called Les Paillers; for the future he spent only the winter months in Paris. His novels became fewer, but not less carefully prepared; he enjoyed a veritable triumph with "Monsieur de Camors" in 1867. Next year he was appointed Royal Librarian at Fontainebleau, an office which he held till the fall of the Empire. He then retired to Les Paillers again, where he had written "Julia de Trécœur" in 1868. The end of his life was troubled by domestic bereavement and loss of health; he hurried restlessly from place to place, a prey to constant nervous agitation. His later writings were numerous, but had not the vitality of those previously mentioned. Octave Feuillet died in Paris, December 28, 1890, and was succeeded at the French Academy by Pierre Loti. Octave was the type of a sensitive, somewhat melancholy fine gentleman; he was very elegant in manners, reserved and ceremonious in society, where he held himself somewhat remote in the radiance of his delicate wit; but within the bosom of his family he was tenderly and almost pathetically demonstrative. The least criticism was torture to him, and it is said that when his comedy of "La Belle au Bois Dormant" was hissed off the boards of the Vaudeville in 1865, for three weeks afterward the life of Feuillet was in danger. Fortunately, however, for a "fiery particle" so sensitive, the greater part of his career was one continuous triumph.*

E. G.

CONTENTS

THE ROMANCE OF A POOR YOUNG MAN

Sursum corda!

PARIS, *April 25, 185–.*

THE second evening I have passed in this miserable room, staring gloomily at the bare hearth, hearing the dull monotone of the street, and feeling more lonely, more forsaken, and nearer to despair in the heart of this great city than a shipwrecked man shivering on a broken plank in mid-ocean.

I have done with cowardice. I will look my destiny in the face till it loses its spectral air. I will open my sorrowful heart to the one confidant whose pity will not hurt, to that pale last friend who looks back at me from the glass. I will write down my thoughts and my life, not in trivial and childish detail, but without serious omissions, and above all without lies. I shall love my journal; it will be a brotherly echo to cheat my loneliness, and at the same time a second conscience warning me not to allow anything to enter into my life which I dare not write down calmly with my own hand.

Now, with sad eagerness I search the past for the facts and incidents which should have long since enlightened me, had not filial respect, habit, and the indifference of a happy idler blinded me. I understand now my mother's deep and constant melancholy; I understand her distaste for society, and why she wore that plain, unvaried dress which sometimes called forth sarcasms, sometimes wrath from my father.—"You look like a servant," he would say to her.

I could not but be conscious that our family life was broken by more serious quarrels, though I was never an actual witness of them. All I heard were my father's sharp and imperious tones, the murmur of a pleading voice, and stifled sobs. These outbursts I attributed to my father's violent and fruitless attempts to revive in my mother the taste for the elegant and brilliant life which she had once enjoyed as much as becomes a virtuous woman, but into which she now accompanied my father with a repugnance that grew stronger every day. After such crises, my father nearly always ran off to buy some costly trinket which my mother found in her table-napkin at dinner, and never wore. One day in the middle of winter she received a large box of rare flowers from Paris; she thanked my father warmly, but directly he had left the room, I saw her slightly raise her shoulders and look up to heaven with an expression of hopeless despair.

During my childhood and early youth I had a great respect for my father, but not much affection. Indeed, throughout this period I saw only the sombre side of his character—the one side that showed itself in domestic life, for which he was not fitted. Later, when I was old enough to go out with him, I was surprised and charmed to find in him a person perfectly new to me. It seemed as if, in our old family house, he felt himself constrained by some fatal spell; once beyond its doors, his forehead cleared, his chest expanded, and he was young again. "Now, Maxime," he would cry, "now for a gallop!" And joyously we would rush along. His shouts of youthful pleasure, his enthusiasm, his fantastic wit, his bursts of feeling, charmed my young heart, and I longed to bring something of all this back to my poor mother, forgotten in her corner at home. I began to love my father; and when I saw all the sympathetic qualities of his brilliant nature displayed in all the functions of social life—at hunts and races, balls and dinners—my fondness for him became an actual admiration. A perfect horseman, a dazzling talker, a bold gambler, daring and open-handed, he became for me the finished type of manly grace and chivalrous nobility. Indeed, he would speak of himself—smiling with some bitterness—as the last of the gentlemen.

Such was my father in society; but as soon as he returned to his home my mother and I saw only a restless, morose, and violent old man.

My father's outbursts to a creature so sweet and delicate as my mother would certainly have revolted me had they not been followed by the quick returns of tenderness and the redoubled attentions I have mentioned. Justified in my eyes by these proofs of penitence, my father seemed to be only a naturally kind, warm-hearted man sometimes irritated beyond endurance by an obstinate and systematic opposition to all his tastes and preferences. I thought my mother was suffering from some nervous derangement. My father gave me to understand so, though, and as I thought very properly, he only referred to this subject with great reserve.

I could not understand what were my mother's feelings towards my father; they were—for me—beyond analysis or definition. Sometimes a strange severity glittered in the looks she fixed on him; but it was only a flash, and the next moment her beautiful soft eyes and her unchanged face showed nothing but tender devotion and passionate submission.

My mother had been married at fifteen, and I was nearly twenty-two when my sister, my poor Hélène, was born. One morning soon afterwards my father came out of my mother's room looking anxious. He signed to me to follow him into the garden.

"Maxime," he said, after walking in silence for a little, "your mother gets stranger and stranger."

"She is so ill just now, father."

"Yes, of course. But now she has the oddest fancy: she wants you to study law."

"Law! What! Does my mother want me, at my age, with my birth and position, to sit among school-boys on the forms of a college class-room? It is absurd."

"So I think," said my father dryly, "but your mother is ill, and—there's no more to be said."

I was a young puppy then, puffed up by my name, my importance, and my little drawing-room successes; but I was sound at heart, and I worshipped my mother, with whom I had lived for twenty years in the closest intimacy possible between two human souls. I hastened to assure her of my obedience; she thanked me with a sad smile and made me kiss my sister who was sleeping on her lap.

We lived about a mile and a half from Grenoble, so I could attend the law classes at the university without leaving home. Day by day my mother followed my progress with such intense and persistent interest that I could not help thinking that she had some stronger motive than the fancy of an invalid; that perhaps my father's hatred and contempt for the practical and tedious side of life might have brought about a certain embarrassment in our affairs which, my mother thought, a knowledge of law and a business training would enable me to put right. This explanation did not satisfy me. No doubt my father had often complained bitterly of our losses during the Revolution, but his complaints had long ceased, and I had never thought them well-founded, because, as far as I could see, our position was in every way satisfactory.

We lived near Grenoble in our hereditary château, which was famous in our country as an aristocratic and lordly dwelling. My father and I have often shot or hunted for a whole day without going off our own land or out of our own woods. Our stables were vast, and filled with expensive horses of which my father was very fond and very proud. Besides, we had a town-house in Paris on the Boulevard des Capucines, where comfortable quarters were always reserved for occasional visits. And nothing in our ordinary way of living could suggest either a small income or close management. Even as regards the table, my father insisted upon a particular degree of delicacy and refinement.

My mother's health declined almost imperceptibly. In time there came an alteration in her disposition. The mouth which, at all events in my presence, had spoken only kind words, grew bitter and aggressive. Every step I took beyond the house provoked a sarcasm. My father was not spared, and bore these attacks with a patience that seemed to me exemplary, but he got more and more into the habit of living away from home. He told me that he must have distraction and amusement. He always wanted me to go with him, and my love of pleasure, and the eagerness of youth, and, to speak truly, my lack of moral courage, made me obey him too readily.

In September, 185–, there were some races near the château, and several of my father's horses were to run. We started early and lunched on the course. About the middle of the day, as I was riding by the course watching the fortunes of a race, one of our men came up and said he had been looking for me for more than half an hour. He added that my father had already been sent for and had gone back to my mother at the château, and that he wanted me to follow him at once.

"But what in Heaven's name is the matter?"

"I think madame is worse," said the servant.

I set off like a madman.

When I reached home my sister was playing on the lawn in the middle of the great, silent courtyard. As I dismounted, she ran up to embrace me, and said, with an air of importance and mystery that was almost joyful:

"The curé has come."

I did not, however, perceive any unusual animation in the house, nor any signs of disorder or alarm. I went rapidly up the staircase, and had passed through the boudoir which communicated with my mother's room, when the door opened softly, and my father appeared. I stopped in front of him; he was very pale, and his lips were trembling.

"Maxime," he said, without looking at me, "your mother is asking for you."

I wished to question him, but he checked me with a gesture, and walked hurriedly towards a window, as if to look out. I entered. My mother lay half-reclining in an easy-chair, one of her arms hanging limply over the side. Again I saw on her face, now as white as wax, the exquisite sweetness and delicate grace which lately had been driven away by suffering. Already the Angel of Eternal Rest was casting the shadow of his wing over that peaceful brow. I fell upon my knees; she half-opened her eyes, raised her drooping head with an effort, and enveloped me in a long, loving look. Then, in a voice which was scarcely more than a broken sigh, she slowly spoke these words:

"Poor child! . . . I am worn out, you see! Do not weep. You have deserted me a little lately, but I have been so trying. We shall meet again, Maxime, and we shall understand one another, my son. I can't say any more. . . . Remind your father of his promise to me. . . . And you, Maxime, be strong in the battle of life, and forgive the weak."

She seemed to be exhausted, and stopped for a moment. Then, raising a finger with difficulty, and looking at me fixedly, she said: "Your sister!"

Her livid eyelids closed; then suddenly she opened them, and threw out her arms with a rigid and sinister gesture. I uttered a cry; my father came quickly, and, with heartrending sobs, pressed the poor martyr's body to his bosom.

Some weeks later, at the formal request of my father, who said that he was obeying the last wishes of her whom we mourned, I left France, and began that wandering life which I have led nearly up to this day. During a year's absence my heart, becoming more affectionate as the selfish frenzy of youth burnt out, urged me to return and renew my life at its source, between my mother's tomb and my sister's cradle. But my father had fixed the duration of my travels, and he had not brought me up to treat his wishes lightly. He wrote to me affectionately, though briefly, showing no desire to hasten my return. So I was the more alarmed when I arrived at Marseilles, two months ago, and found several letters from him, all feverishly begging me to return at once.

It was on a sombre February evening, that I saw once more the massive walls of our ancient house standing out against the light veil of snow that lay upon the country. A sharp north wind blew in icy gusts; flakes of frozen sleet dropped like dead leaves from the trees of the avenue, and struck the wet soil with a faint and plaintive sound. As I entered the court a shadow, which I took to be my father's, fell upon a window of the large drawing-room on the ground floor—a room which had not been used during my mother's last days. I hurried on, and my father, seeing me, gave a hoarse cry, then opened his arms to me, and I felt his heart beating wildly against my own.

"Thou art frozen, my poor child," he said, much against his habit, for he seldom addressed me in the second person. "Warm thyself, warm thyself. This is a cold room, but I prefer it now; at least one can breathe here."

"Are you well, father?"

"Pretty well, as you see."

Leaving me by the fireplace, he resumed his walk across the vast *salon*, dimly lighted by two or three candles. I seemed to have interrupted this walk of his. This strange welcome alarmed me. I looked at my father in dull surprise.

"Have you seen my horses?" he said suddenly, without stopping.

"But, father——"

"Ah, yes, of course, you've only just come." After a silence he continued. "Maxime," he said, "I have something to tell you."

"I'm listening, father."

He did not seem to hear me, but walked about a little, and kept on repeating, "I have something to tell you, my son." At last he sighed deeply, passed his hand across his forehead, and sitting down suddenly, signed to me to take a seat opposite to him. Then, as if he wanted to speak and had not the courage to do so, his eyes rested on mine, and I read in them an expression of suffering, humility, and supplication that in a man so proud as my father touched me deeply. Whatever the faults he found it so hard to confess, I felt from the bottom of my heart that he was fully pardoned.

Suddenly his eyes, which had never left mine, were fixed in an astonished stare, vague and terrible. His hand stiffened on my arm; he raised himself in his chair, then drooped, and in an instant fell heavily on the floor. He was dead.

The heart does not reason or calculate. That is its glory. In a moment I had divined everything. One minute had been enough to show me—all at once, and without a word of explanation—in a burst of irresistible light, the fatal truth which a thousand things daily repeated under my eyes had never made me suspect. Ruin was here, in this house, over my head. Yet I do not think that I should have mourned my father more sincerely or more bitterly if he had left me loaded with benefits. With my regret and my deep sorrow there was mingled a pity, strangely poignant in that it was the pity of a son for his father. That beseeching, humbled, hopeless look haunted me. Bitterly I regretted that I had not been able to speak a word of consolation to that heart before it broke! Wildly I called to him who could no longer hear me, "I forgive you, I forgive you." My God, what moments were these! As far as I have been able to guess, my mother, when she was dying, had made my father promise to sell the greater part of his property; to pay off the whole of the enormous debt he had incurred by spending every year a third more than his income, and to live solely and strictly on what he had left. My father had tried to keep to this engagement; he had sold the timber and part of the estate, but finding himself master of a considerable capital, he had applied only a small portion of it to the discharge of his debts, and had attempted to restore our fortunes by staking the remainder in the hateful chances of the Stock Exchange. He had thus completed his ruin. I have not yet sounded the depths of the abyss in which we are engulfed. A week after my father's death

I was taken seriously ill, and after two months of suffering I was only just able to leave my ancient home on the day that a stranger took possession of it. Fortunately an old friend of my mother's, who lives at Paris, and who formerly acted as notary to our family, has come to my help. He has offered to undertake the work of liquidation which to my inexperienced judgment seemed beset with unconquerable difficulties. I left the whole business to him, and I presume that now his work is completed. I went to his house directly I arrived yesterday; he was in the country, and will not return till to-morrow.

These have been two cruel days; uncertainty is the worst of all evils, because it is the only one that necessarily stops the springs of action and checks our courage. I should have been very much surprised if, ten years ago, any one had told me that the old notary, whose formal language and stiff politeness so much amused my father and me, would one day be the oracle from whom I should await the supreme sentence of my destiny.

I do my best to guard against excessive hopes; I have calculated approximately that, after paying all the debts, we should have a hundred and twenty to a hundred and fifty thousand francs left. A fortune of five millions should leave so much salvage at least. I intend to take ten thousand francs and seek my fortune in the new States of America; the rest I shall resign to my sister.

Enough of writing for to-night. Recalling such memories is a mournful occupation. Nevertheless, I feel that it has made me calmer. Work is surely a sacred law, since even the lightest task discharged brings a certain contentment and serenity. Yet man does not love work; he cannot fail to see its good effects; he tastes them every day, and blesses them, and each day he comes to his work with the same reluctance. I think that is a singular and mysterious contradiction, as if in toil we felt at once a chastisement, and the divine and fatherly hand of the chastiser.

Thursday.

When I woke this morning a letter from old M. Laubépin was brought to me. He invited me to dinner and apologized for taking such a liberty. He said nothing about my affairs. I augured unfavourably from this silence.

In the meantime I fetched my sister from her convent, and took her about Paris. The child knows nothing of our ruin. In the course of the day she had some rather expensive fancies. She provided herself liberally with gloves, pink notepaper, bonbons for her friends, delicate scents, special soaps, and tiny pencils, all very necessary useful things, but not as necessary as a dinner. May she never have to realize this!

At six o'clock I was at M. Laubépin's in the Rue Cassette. I do not know our old friend's age, but to-day I found him looking just the same as ever—tall and thin, with a little stoop, untidy white hair, and piercing eyes under bushy black eyebrows—altogether a face at once strong and subtle. I recognised the unvarying costume, the old-fashioned black coat, the professional white cravat, the family diamond in the shirt-frill—in short, all the outward signs of a serious, methodical, and conservative nature. The old gentleman was waiting for me at the open door of his little *salon*. After making me a low bow, he took my hand lightly between two of his fingers and conducted me to a homely looking old lady who was standing by the fire-place.

"The Marquis de Champcey d'Hauterive!" said M. Laubépin, in his strong, rich, and emphatic voice, and turning quickly to me, added in a humbler tone, "Mme. Laubépin!"

We sat down. An awkward silence ensued. I had expected an immediate explanation of my position. Seeing that this was to be postponed,

I assumed at once that it was unfavourable, an assumption confirmed by the discreet and compassionate glances with which Mme. Laubépin furtively honoured me. As for M. Laubépin, he observed me with a remarkable attention not altogether kindly. My father, I remember, always maintained that at the bottom of his heart and under his respectful manner the ceremonious old scrivener had a little of *bourgeois* democratic and even Jacobin leaven. It seemed to me that this leaven was working just now, and that the old man found some satisfaction for his secret antipathies in the spectacle of a gentleman under torture. In spite of my real depression, I began to talk at once, trying to appear quite unconcerned.

"So, M. Laubépin," I said, "you've left the Place des Petits-Pères, the dear old Place. How could you bring yourself to do it? I would never have believed it of you."

"*Mon Dieu*, marquis," replied M. Laubépin, "I must admit that it is an infidelity unbecoming at my age; but in giving up the practice I had to give up my chambers as well, for one can't carry off a notary's plate as one can a sign-board."

"But you still undertake some business?"

"Yes, in a friendly way, marquis. Some of the honourable families, the important families, whose confidence I have had the good fortune to secure in the course of forty-five years of practice, are still glad, especially in situations of unusual delicacy, to have the benefit of my experience, and I believe I may say they rarely regret having followed my advice."

As M. Laubépin finished this testimonial to his own merits, an old servant came in and announced that dinner was served. It was my privilege to conduct Mme. Laubépin into the adjacent dining-room. Throughout the meal the conversation never rose above the most ordinary commonplaces. M. Laubépin continued to look at me in the same penetrating and ambiguous manner, while Mme. Laubépin offered me each dish in the mournful and compassionate tone we use at the bedside of an invalid. In time we left the table, and the old notary took me into his study, where coffee was served immediately. He made me sit down, and standing before the fire-place, began:

"Marquis," he said, "you have done me the honour of intrusting to me the administration of the estate of your father, the late Marquis de Champcey d'Hauterive. Yesterday I was about to write to you, when I learned of your arrival in Paris. This enables me to convey to you, *vivâ voce*, the result of my zeal and of my action."

"I foresee, M. Laubépin, that the result is not favourable."

"Marquis, it is not favourable, and you will need all your courage to bear it. But it is my rule to proceed methodically.—In the year 1820 Mlle. Louise Hélène Dugald Delatouche d'Erouville was sought in marriage by Charles-Christian Odiot, Marquis de Champcey d'Hauterive. A tradition a century old had placed the management of the Dugald Delatouche affairs in my hands, and I was further permitted a respectful intimacy with the young heiress of the house. I thought it my duty, therefore, to oppose her infatuation by every argument in my power and to dissuade her from this deplorable alliance. I say deplorable alliance without reference to M. de Champcey's fortune, which was nearly equal to that of Mlle. Delatouche, though even at this time he had mortgaged it to some extent. I say so because I knew his character and temperament, which were in the main hereditary. Under the fascinating and chivalrous manner common to all of his race I saw clearly the heedless obstinacy, the incurable irresponsibility, the mania for pleasure, and, finally, the pitiless selfishness."

"Sir," I interrupted sharply, "my father's memory is sacred to me, and so it must be to every one who speaks of him in my presence."

"Sir," replied the old man with a sudden and violent emotion, "I respect that sentiment, but when I speak of your father I find it hard to forget that he was the man who killed your mother, that heroic child, that saint, that angel!"

I had risen in great agitation. M. Laubépin, who had taken a few steps across the room, seized my arm. "Forgive me, young man," he said to me. "I loved your mother and wept for her. You must forgive me." Then returning to the fire-place, he continued in his usual solemn tone:

"I had the honour and the pain of drawing up your mother's marriage contract.

"In spite of my remonstrance, the strict settlement of her property upon herself had not been adopted, and it was only with much difficulty that I got included in the deed a protective clause by which about a third of your mother's estate could not be sold, except with her consent duly and legally authenticated. A useless precaution, marquis; I might call it the cruel precaution of an ill-advised friendship. This fatal clause brought most intolerable sufferings to the very person whose peace it was intended to secure. I refer to the disputes and quarrels and wrangles the echo of which must sometimes have reached your ears, and in which, bit by bit, your mother's last heritage—her children's bread—was torn from her!"

"Spare me, M. Laubépin!"

"I obey. . . . I will speak only of the present. Directly I was honoured with your confidence, marquis, my first duty was to advise you not to accept the encumbered estate unless after paying all liabilities."

"Such a course seemed to cast a slur on my father's memory, and I could not adopt it."

M. Laubépin darted one of his inquisitorial glances at me, and continued:

"You are apparently aware that by not having availed yourself of this perfectly legal method, you became responsible for all liabilities, even if they exceed the value of the estate itself. And that, it is my painful duty to tell you, is the case in the present instance. You will see by these documents that after getting exceptionally favourable terms for the town-house, you and your sister are still indebted to your father's creditors to the amount of forty-five thousand francs."

I was utterly stunned by this news, which far exceeded my worst apprehensions. For a minute

I stared at the clock without seeing the hour it marked, and listened dazed to the monotonous sound of the pendulum.

"Now," continued M. Laubépin, after a silence, "the moment has come to tell you, marquis, that your mother, in view of contingencies which are unfortunately realized to-day, deposited with me some jewels which are valued at about fifty thousand francs. To exempt this small sum, now your sole resource, from the claims of the creditors of the estate, we can, I believe, make use of the legal resource which I shall have the honour of submitting to you."

"That will not be necessary, M. Laubépin. I am only too glad to be able, through this unexpected means, to pay my father's debts in full, and I beg you to devote it to that purpose."

M. Laubépin bowed slightly.

"As you wish, marquis," he said, "but I must point out to you that when this deduction has been made, the joint fortune of Mlle. Hélène and yourself will consist of something like four or five thousand livres, which, at the present rate of interest, will give you an income of two hundred and twenty-five francs. That being so, may I venture to ask in a confidential, friendly, and respectful way whether you have thought of any way of providing for your own existence and for that of your ward and sister? And, generally, what your plans are?"

"I tell you frankly I have none. Whatever plans I may have had are quite impossible in the state of destitution to which I am now reduced. If I were alone in the world I should enlist, but I have my sister, and I cannot endure the thought of seeing the poor child subjected to toil and privations. She is happy in the convent and young enough to stay there some years longer. I would gladly accept any employment which would enable me, by the strictest personal economy, to pay her expenses each year and provide for her dowry in the future."

M. Laubépin looked hard at me.

"At your age, marquis, you must not expect," he replied, "to achieve that praiseworthy object by entering the slow ranks of public officials and governmental functionaries. You require an appointment which will assure you from the outset a yearly revenue of five or six thousand francs. And I must also tell you that this desideratum is not, in the present state of our social organization, to be obtained by simply holding out your hand. Happily, I am in a position to make some propositions to you which are likely to modify your present situation immediately and without much trouble."

M. Laubépin fixed his eyes on me more penetratingly than ever.

"In the first place, marquis," he went on, "I am the mouthpiece of a clever, rich, and influential speculator. This personage has originated an idea for an important undertaking, the nature of which will be explained to you at a later period. Its success largely depends on the co-operation of the aristocracy of this country. He believes that an old and illustrious name like yours, marquis, appearing among the originators of the enterprise, would have great weight with the special public to whom the prospectus will be addressed. In return for this service, he engages to hand over to you a certain number of fully paid-up shares, which are now valued at ten thousand francs, and which will be worth two or three times that amount when the affair is well launched. In addition, he——"

"That is enough, M. Laubépin. Such infamies are unworthy of the trouble you take in mentioning them."

For a moment I saw his eyes flash and sparkle. The stiff folds in his face relaxed as he smiled faintly.

"If you do not approve of this proposition, marquis," he said unctuously, "neither do I. However, I thought it was my duty to submit it for your consideration. Here is another, which, perhaps, will please you more, and which is really more attractive. One of my oldest clients is a worthy merchant who has lately retired from business, and now passes his life with an only and much-loved daughter, in the quiet enjoyment of an *aurea mediocritas* of twenty-five thousand francs a year. Two or three days ago my client's daughter, by some accident, heard of your position. I thought it right—indeed, to speak frankly, I was at some trouble—to ascertain that the young lady would not hesitate for a moment to accept the title of Marquise de Champcey. Her appearance is agreeable, and she has many excellent qualities. Her father approves. I await only a word from you, marquis, to tell you the name and residence of this interesting family."

"M. Laubépin, this quite decides me; from to-morrow I shall cease to use a title which is ridiculous for one in my position, and which, it seems, makes me the object of the most paltry intrigues. My family name is Odiot, and henceforth I shall use no other. And now, though I recognise gratefully the keen interest in my welfare which has induced you to be the channel of such remarkable propositions, I must beg you to spare me any others of a like character."

"In that case, marquis, I have absolutely nothing more to tell you," said M. Laubépin, and, as if suddenly taken with a fit of joviality, he rubbed his hands together with a noise like the crackling of parchment.

"You are a difficult man to place, M. Maxime," he added, smiling. "Oh, very difficult! It is remarkable that I should not have already noticed your striking likeness to your mother, particularly your eyes and your smile . . . but we must not digress; and, since you are resolved to maintain yourself by honest work, may I ask what are your talents and qualifications?"

"My education, monsieur, was naturally that of a man destined for a life of wealth and ease. However, I have studied law, and am nominally a barrister."

"A barrister! The devil you are! But the name is not enough. At the bar, more than in any other career, everything depends on personal effort; and now—let us see—do you speak well, marquis?"

"So badly that I believe I am incapable of putting two sentences together in public."

"H'm! Scarcely what one could call a heaven-born orator. You must try something else; but the matter requires more careful consideration. I see you are tired, marquis. Here are your papers, which you can examine at your leisure. I have the honour to wish you farewell. Allow me to light you down. A moment—am I to await your further instructions before applying the value of those jewels to the payment of your creditors?"

"Oh, by no means. But I should wish you rather to deduct a just remuneration for your kind exertions."

We had reached the landing of the staircase; M. Laubépin, who stooped a little as he walked, sharply straightened himself.

"So far as your creditors are concerned," he said, "you may count upon my obedience, marquis. As to me, I was your mother's friend, and I beg humbly but earnestly that her son will treat me as a friend."

I gave my hand to the old gentleman; he shook it warmly and we parted.

Back in the little room I now occupy, under the roof of the *hôtel*, which is mine no longer, I wished to convince myself that the full knowledge of my misery had not depressed me to a degree unworthy of a man. So I have sat down to write an account of this decisive day of my life, endeavouring to preserve exactly the phraseology of the old notary, a mixture of stiffness and courtesy, of mistrust and kind feeling, which more than once made me smile, though my heart was bleeding.

I am face to face with poverty. Not the haughty, hidden, and poetic poverty that among forests and deserts and savannas fired my imagination, but actual misery, need, dependence, humiliation, and something worse even—the poverty of the rich man who has fallen; poverty in a decent coat; the poverty that hides its ungloved hands from the former friends it passes in the street. Come, brother, courage, courage . . . !

Monday, April 27th.

For five days I have been waiting in vain for news of M. Laubépin. I had counted considerably on the interest that he had appeared to feel in me. His experience, his business connections, and the number of people he knows, would enable him to be of service to me. I was ready to take all necessary steps under his direction, but, left to myself, I do not know which way to turn. I thought he was one of the men who promise little and do much. I am afraid that I have been mistaken. This morning I determined to go to his house on the pretext of returning the papers he had given me, after verifying their dreary exactitude. I was told that he had gone to enjoy a taste of country life at some château in the heart of Brittany. He would be away two or three days longer. I was completely taken aback. I had not only the pain of finding indifference and desertion where I had looked for the readiness of devoted friendship, I had, in addition, the bitter disappointment of returning, as I went, with an empty purse. I had, in fact, intended to ask M. Laubépin to advance me some money from the three or four thousand francs due to us after full payment of our debts. In vain have I lived like an anchorite since I came to Paris. The small sum I had reserved for my journey is completely exhausted—so completely that, after making a truly pastoral breakfast this morning—*castaneæ molles et pressi copia lactis*—I was obliged to have recourse to a kind of trickery for my dinner to-night. I will make melancholy record of it here.

The less one has had for breakfast, the more one wants for dinner. I had felt all the force of this axiom long before the sun had finished its course. Among the strollers whom the mild air had attracted to the Tuileries this afternoon to watch the first smiles of spring playing on the faces of the marble fauns, the observant might have noted a young man of irreproachable appearance who seemed to study the awakening of nature with extraordinary interest. Not satisfied with devouring the fresh verdure with his eyes, he would furtively detach the young, appetizing shoots and the half-opened leaves from their stems, and put them to his lips with the curiosity of a botanist. I convinced myself in this way that this form of nourishment, suggested by accounts of shipwrecks, is of very little value. Still, I enriched my experience with some interesting discoveries: for instance, I know now that the foliage of the chestnut has an exceedingly bitter taste; that the rose is not unpleasant; that the lime is oily and rather agreeable; the lilac pungent—and I believe unwholesome.

Meditating on these discoveries, I walked towards Hélène's convent. I found the parlour as crowded as a hive, and I was more than usually bewildered by the tumultuous confidences of the young bees. Hélène arrived, her hair in disorder, her cheeks flushed, her eyes red and sparkling. In her hand she had a piece of bread as long as her arm. As she embraced me in an absent way, I asked:

"Well, little girl, what is the matter? You've been crying."

"No, Maxime, no, it's nothing."

"Well, what is it? Now tell me. . . ."

In a lower tone she said:

"Oh, I am very miserable, dear Maxime!"

"Really? Tell me all about it while you eat your bread."

"Oh, I shall certainly not eat my bread. I am too miserable to eat. You know Lucy—Lucy Campbell, my dearest friend. Well, we've quarrelled completely."

"Oh, *mon Dieu!* Don't worry, darling, you'll make it up. It will be all right, dear."

"Oh, Maxime, that's impossible. It was such a serious quarrel. It was nothing at first, but you know one gets excited and loses one's head. Listen, Maxime! We were playing battledore, and Lucy made a mistake about the score. I was six hundred and eighty, and she was only six hundred and fifteen, and she declared she was six hundred and sixty-five! You must say that was a little too bad. Of course I said my figure was right, and she said hers was. 'Well, mademoiselle,' I said to her, 'let us ask these young ladies. I appeal to them.' 'No, mademoiselle,' she replied, 'I am sure I am right, and you don't play fair.' 'And—and you, mademoiselle,' I said to her—'you are a liar!' 'Very well, mademoiselle,' she said then, 'I despise you too much to answer you.' Just at that moment Sister Sainte-Félix came up, which was a good thing, for I am sure I should have hit her. Now, you know what happened. Can we possibly make it up? No, it is impossible; it would be cowardly. But I can't tell you how I suffer. I don't believe there's any one in the world so miserable as I am."

"Yes, dear, it's difficult to imagine anything more distressing; but it seems to me that you partly brought it on yourself, for it was you who used the most offensive word. Tell me, is Lucy in the parlour?"

"Yes, there she is, in the corner."

With a dignified and careful movement of her head she indicated a very fair little girl. Her cheeks, too, were flushed, and her eyes were red. Apparently she was giving an account of the drama, which Sister Sainte-Félix had so fortunately interrupted, to an old lady who was listening attentively.

Mlle. Lucy, while she talked with an earnestness appropriate to the subject, kept looking furtively at Hélène and me.

"Dear child," I said to Hélène, "do you trust me?"

"Yes, Maxime, I trust you very much."

"In that case I will tell you what to do. Go very gently behind Mlle. Lucy's chair; take her head in your hands—like this, when she is not looking—and kiss her on both cheeks—like this, with all your might—and then you will see what she will do in her turn."

For a second or two Hélène seemed to hesitate; then she set off at a great rate, fell like a thunder-clap on Mlle. Campbell, but nevertheless gave her the sweetest of surprises. The two young sufferers, at last eternally united, mingled their tears in a touching group, while the respectable old Mrs. Campbell blew her nose with a noise as of a bagpipe.

Hélène came back to me radiant.

"Well, dear," I said, "I hope you're going to eat your bread now."

"Oh, no! I can't, Maxime. I am too much excited, and—besides, I must tell you—to-day a new pupil came and gave us quite a feast of meringues, éclairs, and chocolate-creams, and I am not a bit hungry. And I am in a great difficulty about it, because when we're not hungry we have to put our bread back in the basket, and in my trouble I forgot, and I shall be punished. But, Maxime, as we're crossing the court when you go, I shall try to drop it down the cellar without any one seeing."

"What, little sister!" I said, colouring a little, "you are going to waste that large piece of bread?"

"It isn't good of me I know, because, perhaps, there are poor people who would be very glad of it, aren't there, Maxime?"

"There certainly are, dear."

"But what do you want me to do? The poor people don't come in here."

"Look here, Hélène, give me the bread, and I'll give it in your name to the first poor man I meet. Will you?"

"Oh, yes!"

The bell rang for school. I broke the bread in two and hid the pieces shamefacedly in my great-coat pockets.

"Dear Maxime," said my sister, "you'll come again soon, won't you? Then you'll tell me whether you met a poor man and gave him my bread, and whether he liked it? Good-bye, Maxime."

"Yes, Hélène, I met a poor man and gave him your bread, which he seized and carried off to his solitary garret, and he liked it. But this poor man had not courage, for he wept as he ate the food that had come from your dear little hands. I will tell you all this, Hélène, because it is good for you to know that there are sufferings more serious than your childish woes. I will tell you everything, except the name of the poor man."

Tuesday, April 28th.

At nine o'clock this morning I called at M. Laubépin's in the vague hope that he might have returned earlier than he intended, but he is not expected until to-morrow. I thought at once of seeing Mme. Laubépin and explaining the awkward position I was placed in through her husband's absence. While I hesitated in a conflict of shame and necessity, the old servant, alarmed, perhaps, by my hungry gaze, settled the question by suddenly shutting the door. I made up my mind hereupon to fast until the next day. After all, I said to myself, a day's abstinence does not kill one. If this showed an excessive pride, at all events I was the only one to suffer, and consequently it concerned no one but myself. I accordingly made my way to the Sorbonne, where I attended several lectures, trying to fill up my corporeal vacuum by spiritual sustenance. But when this resource came to an end I found it had been quite inadequate. And I had an attack of nervous irritation which I tried to calm by walking. It was a cold, misty day. As I crossed the Pont des Saints-Pères I stopped for a minute in spite of myself. Leaning on the parapet, I watched the troubled water rushing under the arches. I know not what unholy thoughts shot through my worn and weakened brain. I saw in the gloomiest colours a future of ceaseless struggle, of dependence, and of humiliation, which I was approaching by the dark gate of hunger; I felt a profound and utter disgust of life; it seemed impossible to me under such conditions. At the same time a flame of fierce and brutal anger leaped up in me. Dazed and reeling, I hung over the void, and saw all the river glittering with sparks of fire.

I will not say, as is usual, God would not have it so. I hate these cant phrases, and I dare to say *I* would not. God has made us free, and if ever before I had doubted it, this supreme moment—when soul and body, courage and cowardice, good and evil, held mortal combat within me—would have swept my doubts away forever.

Master of myself again, those terrible waves

only suggested an innocent, and rather absurd longing to quench the thirst that tortured me. I soon remembered that I should find much purer water in my room at home. I went quickly towards the *hôtel*, imagining that the most delicious pleasures awaited me there. With pathetic childishness I delighted in this glorious device, and wondered I had not thought of it sooner. On the boulevard I suddenly came face to face with Gaston de Vaux, whom I had not seen for two years. After a moment's hesitation he stopped, grasped my hand cordially, said a word or two about my travels, and left me hurriedly. But he turned back.

"My friend," he said to me, "you must allow me to let you share a piece of good luck I've just had. I have put my hand on a treasure; I have got some cigars which cost me two francs each, but really they are beyond price. Here's one; you must tell me how you like it. *Au revoir*, old man!"

Wearily I mounted the six flights to my room, and trembling with emotion, I seized my friendly water-bottle and swallowed the contents in small mouthfuls. Afterward I lighted my friend's cigar, and smiled encouragement at myself in the glass. Feeling that movement and the distraction of the streets were good for me, I went out again directly. Opening my door, I was surprised and annoyed to see the wife of the concierge of the *hôtel* standing in the narrow corridor. My sudden appearance seemed to disconcert her. This woman had formerly been in my mother's service, and had become a favourite with her, and when she married, my mother had given her the profitable post she still held. For some days I had an idea that she was watching me, and now, having nearly caught her in the act, I asked her roughly what she wanted.

"Oh, nothing, M. Maxime, nothing," she replied, much confused. "I was seeing to the gas."

I shrugged my shoulders and went away.

Night was falling, so I could walk about in the more frequented places without being fearful of awkward recognitions. I was obliged to throw away my cigar—it made me feel sick. My promenade lasted two or three hours, and painful hours they were. There is something peculiarly poignant in feeling oneself attacked, in the midst of the brilliance and plenty of civilization, by the scourge of savage life—hunger. It brings you near to madness. It's a tiger springing at your throat in the middle of the boulevards.

I made some original reflections. Hunger,

after all, is not an empty word. There actually is a complaint of that name, and there are human beings who endure nearly every day what through a mere accident I am suffering for once in my life. And how many have their misery embittered by troubles which I am spared! I know that the one being in the world whom I love is sheltered from such sufferings as mine. But how many cannot suffer alone; how many must hear the heart-rending cry of nature repeated on beloved lips that ask for food; how many for whom pale women and unsmiling children are waiting in bare cold rooms! Poor creatures! Blessed be holy charity!

After these thoughts I dared not complain; they gave me courage to bear my trial to the end. As a matter of fact I could have shortened it. There are two or three restaurants where I am known, and where, when I was rich, I had often gone in without hesitation, though I had forgotten to bring my purse. I might have made some such pretext. Nor would it have been difficult for me to borrow a franc or two in Paris. But I recoiled from such expedients. They suggested poverty too plainly, and they came too near to trickery. That descent is swift and slippery for the poor, and I believe I would rather lose honesty itself than the delicacy which gives distinction to the commonplace virtue. I have seen too often with what facility this exquisite sentiment of honesty loses its bloom, even in the finest natures, not merely under the breath of misery, but at the slightest contact with privation. So I shall keep strict watch over myself. I shall be on my guard henceforth against even the most innocent compromise with conscience. When bad times come, do not accustom your soul to suppleness; it is only too prone to yield.

Fatigue and cold drove me back about nine o'clock. The door of the *hôtel* was open. Treading as lightly as a ghost, I had reached the staircase when the sound of a lively conversation came from the concierge's room. They were talking about me, for at this very moment the tyrant of the house pronounced my name with unmistakable contempt.

"Be good enough, Mme. Vauberger," said the concierge, "not to trouble me with your Maxime. Did I ruin your Maxime? Then what are you talking to me about? If he kills himself, they'll bury him, won't they?"

"I tell you, Vauberger," his wife answered, "it would have made your heart bleed to see him drain his water-bottle. And if I believed you meant what you say in that offhand manner—just like an actor—'If he kills himself, they'll bury him!' I would—— But I know you don't, because you're a good sort, although you don't like being upset. Fancy being without fire or bread! And that after being fed on dainties all your life, and wrapped up in furs like a little pet cat. It's a shame and a disgrace. A nice sort of government yours is to allow such things!"

"But it has nothing to do with the government," said M. Vauberger, reasonably enough. "And I'm sure you're wrong; it's not so bad as all that. He can't be wanting bread; it's impossible."

"All right, Vauberger. I've more to tell you. I've followed him. I've watched him, and made Edouard watch him, too. Yes, I have. I'm certain he had no dinner yesterday, and no breakfast to-day; and as I've searched his pockets and all the drawers, and not found so much as a red cent, you may be sure he hasn't had any dinner to-day, for he's much too high and mighty to go and beg one."

"Oh, is he? So much the worse for him. Poor people shouldn't be proud," said the worthy concierge, true to the sentiments of his calling.

I had had enough of this dialogue, and put an end to it abruptly by opening the door and asking M. Vauberger for a light. I could not have astounded him more if I had asked for his head. Though I particularly wished not to give way before these people, I could not help stumbling once or twice as I went up the stairs. My head was swimming. Usually my room was as cold as ice. Imagine my surprise at finding a bright, cheerful fire, which sent a pleasant warmth through the room. I wasn't stoic enough to put it out, and I blessed the kind hearts there are in the world. I stretched myself out in an old arm-chair of Utrecht velvet, which, like myself, had been brought by reverses from the first floor to the garret. I tried to sleep. For half an hour I had been dreaming in a kind of torpor of sumptuous banquets and merry junketings, when the noise of the door opening made me jump up with a start. I thought I was dreaming still when Mme. Vauberger came in, carrying a big tray with two or three savoury dishes steaming on it. Before I could shake off my lethargy she had put the tray down and had begun to lay the cloth. At last I started up hastily.

"Well," I said, "what does this mean? What are you doing?"

Mme. Vauberger pretended to be greatly surprised.

"I thought you ordered dinner, sir?"

"Oh, no."

"Edouard told me that——"

"Edouard made a mistake; it's for one of the other tenants; you had better see."

"But there's no other tenant on this floor, sir . . . I can't make out . . ."

"Well, it was not for me. What does all this mean? Oh, you annoy me! Take it away."

The poor woman began to fold the cloth, looking at me reproachfully, like a favourite dog who has been beaten.

"I suppose you've had dinner already, sir," she said, timidly.

"No doubt."

"That is a pity, because this dinner is quite ready, and now it will be wasted, and the boy'll get a scolding from his father. If you hadn't had your dinner already, sir, you would have very much obliged me if——"

I stamped my foot violently.

"Leave the room, I tell you," I said, and as she was going out I went up to her. "My good Louison," I said, "I understand, and I thank you; but I am not very well to-night, and I have no appetite."

"Ah, M. Maxime," she exclaimed, in tears, "you don't know how you hurt my feelings. Well, you can pay me for the dinner; you shall if you like; you can give me the money as soon as you get some . . . but if you gave me a hundred thousand francs, it wouldn't make me so happy as seeing you eat my poor dinner. You would do me a great kindness, M. Maxime. You, who are so clever, you ought to understand how I feel. Oh, I know you will, M. Maxime!"

"Well, my dear Louison, what am I to do? I can't give you a hundred thousand francs . . . but . . . I am going to eat your dinner. All by myself, too, if you don't mind."

"Certainly, sir. Oh, thank you, sir; I thank you very much indeed. You have a kind heart, sir."

"And a good appetite, Louison. Give me your hand—oh, not to put money in, you may be sure. There! *Au revoir*, Louison."

The good woman went out sobbing.

I did justice to Louison's dinner, and had just finished writing these lines when a grave and heavy footstep sounded on the stairs, and at the same time I thought I heard the voice of my humble providence whispering confidences in hurried, nervous tones. A moment or two later there was a knock. Louison slipped away in the darkness, and the solemn outline of the old notary appeared in the doorway.

M. Laubépin cast a keen glance at the tray where I had left the fragments of my dinner. Then coming towards me and opening his arms, at once confused and reproachful, he said:

"In Heaven's name, marquis, why did you not——"

He broke off, strode quickly about the room, and then coming to a sudden halt, exclaimed:

"Young man, you had no right to do this; you have given pain to a friend, and you have made an old man blush."

He was much moved. I looked at him, a little moved myself and not knowing what to say, when he suddenly clasped me in his arms and murmured in my ear, "My poor child . . . !"

For a moment we said nothing. When we had sat down, M. Laubépin continued.

"Maxime," he said, "are you in the same mind as when I left you? Have you the courage to accept the humblest work, the least important occupation, provided it is honourable, and that it gives you a livelihood and preserves your sister from the sufferings and dangers of poverty?"

"Most certainly I am; it's my duty, and I am ready to do it."

"Very well, my friend. Now listen to me. I have just returned from Brittany. In that ancient province there is a family called Laroque, who have for many years past honoured me with their entire confidence. This family is now represented by an old man and two ladies whom age or disposition render incapable of business. The Laroques have a substantial income derived from their large estates in land, which have latterly been managed by an agent whom I took the liberty to regard as a rogue. The day following our last interview, Maxime, I received intelligence of the death of this man. I immediately set out for the Château Laroque and asked for the appointment for you. I laid stress on your having been called to the bar, and dwelt particularly on your moral qualities. Respecting your wishes, I did not allude to your birth; you are not, and will not, be known in that house under any name but that of Maxime Odiot. A pavilion at some distance from the house will be allotted to you, and you will be able to have your meals there when, for any reason, you do not care to join the family at table. Your salary will be six thousand francs a year. How will that suit you?"

"It will suit me perfectly. You must let me acknowledge at once how much I feel the consideration and delicacy of your friendship. But to tell you the truth, I am afraid I am rather a strange kind of business man—rather a novice, you know."

"You need have no anxiety on that score, my friend. I anticipated your scruples, and concealed nothing from the parties concerned. 'Madame,' I said to my excellent friend, Mme. Laroque, 'you require an agent and an administrator of your income. I offer you one. He is far from possessing the talents of his predecessor; he is by no means versed in the mysteries of leases and farm-freeholds; he does not know the alphabet of the affairs you are so good as to intrust to him; he has had no experience, no practice, and no opportunity of learning; but he has something which his predecessor lacked, which sixty years of experience had not given him, and which he would not have acquired in ten thousand years—and that is honesty, madame. I have seen him under fire, and I will answer for him. Engage him; he will be indebted to you, and so shall I.' Young man, Mme. Laroque laughed very much at my way of recommending people, but in the end it turned out to be a good way, for it has succeeded."

The worthy old gentleman then offered to impart to me some elementary general notions on the kind of administration I was about to undertake, and to these he added, in connection with the interests of the Laroque family, the results of some inquiries which he had made and put into shape for me.

"And when am I to go, my dear sir?"

"To say the truth, my boy" (he had entirely dropped the "marquis"), "the sooner the better, for those good people could not make out a receipt unaided. My excellent friend, Mme. Laroque, more especially, though an admirable woman in many respects, is beyond conception careless, indiscreet, and childish in business matters. She is a Creole."

"Ah! she is a Creole," I repeated with some vivacity.

"Yes, young man, an old Creole lady," M. Laubépin said dryly. "Her husband was a Breton; but these details will come in good time. . . . Good-bye till to-morrow, Maxime, and be of good cheer. Ah! I had forgotten. On Thursday morning, before my departure, I did something which will be of service to you. Among your creditors there are some rogues, whose relations with your father were obviously usurious. Armed with the thunders of the law, I reduced their claims on my own responsibility, and made them give me receipts in full. So now your capital amounts to twenty thousand francs. Add to this reserve what you are able to save each year from your salary, and in ten years' time we shall have a good dowry for Hélène. Well, well, come and lunch with Maître Laubépin to-morrow, and we will settle all the rest. Good-bye, Maxime; good-night, my dear child!"

"God bless you, sir!"

CHÂTEAU DE LAROQUE (D'ARZ), *May 1st.*

I left Paris yesterday. My last interview with M. Laubépin was painful. I feel the affection of a son for the old man. Then I had to bid Hélène farewell. It was necessary to tell her something of the truth, to make her understand why I was compelled to accept an appointment. I talked vaguely of temporary business difficulties. The poor child understood, I think, more than I had said; her large, wondering eyes filled with tears as she fell upon my neck.

At last I got away. I went by train to

Rennes, where I stayed the night. This morning I took the diligence, which put me down, four or five hours ago, at a little Morbihan town not far from the château of Laroque. We had travelled ten leagues or more from Rennes, and still I had seen nothing to justify the reputed picturesqueness of our ancient Armorica. A flat, green country without variety; eternal apple-trees in eternal fields; ditches and wooded slopes shutting off the view on both sides of the road; here and there a nook full of rural charm, and a few blouses and glazed hats relieving the very ordinary scene. All this strongly inclined me to think that poetic Brittany was merely a pretentious and somewhat pallid sister of Lower Normandy. Tired of disillusions and apple-trees, I had for more than an hour ceased to take any notice of the country. I was dozing heavily, when I felt suddenly that the lumbering vehicle was lurching forward heavily. At the same time the pace of the horses slackened, and a clanking noise, together with a peculiar vibration, proclaimed that the worst of drivers had applied the worst of brakes to the worst of diligences. An old lady clutched my arm with the ready sympathy excited by a sense of common danger. I put my head out of the window; we were descending, between two lofty slopes, an extremely steep hill, evidently the work of an engineer too much enamoured of the straight line.

Half-sliding, half-rolling, we soon reached the bottom of a narrow valley of gloomy aspect. A feeble brook flowed silently and slowly among thick reeds, and over its crumbling banks hung a few moss-grown tree-trunks. The road crossed the stream by a bridge of a single arch, and, climbing the farther hill, cut a white track across a wide, barren, and naked *lande* whose crest stood out sharply against the horizon in front of us. Near the bridge and close to the road was a ruined hovel. Its air of desolation struck to the heart. A young, robust man was splitting wood by the door; his long, fair hair was fastened at the back by a black ribbon. He raised his head, and I was surprised at the strange character of his features and at the calm gaze of his blue eyes. He greeted me in an unknown tongue and with a quiet, soft, and timid accent. A woman was spinning at the cottage window; the style of her hair and dress reproduced with theatrical fidelity the images of those slim châtelaines of stone we see on tombs. These people did not look like peasants; they had, in the highest degree, that easy, gracious, and serious air we call distinction. And they had, too, the sad and dreamy expression often seen among people whose nationality has been destroyed.

I had got down to walk up the hill. The *lande*, which was not separated from the road, extended all round me as far and farther than I could see; stunted furze clung to the black earth on every side; here and there were ravines, clefts, deserted quarries, and low rocks, but no trees.

Only when I had reached the high ground I saw the distant sombre line of the heath broken by a more distant strip of the horizon. A little serrated, blue as the sea and steeped in sunlight, it seemed to open in the midst of this desolation the sudden vision of some radiant fairy region. At last I saw Brittany!

I had to engage a carriage to take me the two leagues that separated me from the end of my journey. During the drive, which was not by any means a rapid one, I vaguely remember seeing woods, glades, lakes, and oases of fresh verdure in the valleys; but as we approached the Château Laroque I was besieged by a thousand apprehensions which left no room for tourist's reflections. In a few minutes I was to enter a strange family on the footing of a sort of servant in disguise, and in a position which would barely secure me the consideration and respect of the lackeys themselves. This was something very new to me. The moment M. Laubépin proposed this post of bailiff, all my instincts, all my habits, had risen in violent protest against the peculiar character of dependence attached to such duties. Nevertheless, I had thought it impossible to refuse without appearing to slight my old friend's zealous efforts on my behalf. Moreover, in a less dependent position, I could not have hoped to obtain for many years the advantages which I should have here from the outset, and which would enable me to work for my sister's future without losing time. I had therefore overcome my repugnance, but it had been very strong, and now revived more strongly than ever in face of the imminent reality. I had need to study once more the articles on duty and sacrifice in the moral code that every man carries in his conscience. At the same time I told myself that there is no situation, however humble, where personal dignity cannot maintain itself—and none, in fact, that it cannot ennoble. Then I sketched out a plan of conduct towards the Laroque family, and promised myself to show a conscientious zeal for their interests, and, to themselves, a just deference equally removed from servility and from stiffness. But I could not conceal from myself that the last part of my task, obviously the most delicate, would be either greatly simplified or complicated by the special characters and dispositions of the people with whom I was to come into contact. Now, M. Laubépin, while recognising that my anxiety on these personal questions was quite legitimate, had been stubbornly sparing of information and details on the subject. However, just as I was starting, he had handed me a private memorandum counselling me at the same time to throw it in the fire as soon as I had profited by its contents. This memorandum I took from my portfolio and proceeded to study its sibylline utterances, which I here reproduce exactly.

"CHÂTEAU DE LAROQUE (D'ARZ)

"LIST OF PERSONS LIVING AT THE AFORESAID CHÂTEAU

"1st. M. Laroque (Louis-Auguste), octogenarian, present head of the family, main source of its wealth: an old sailor, famous under the first empire as a sort of authorized pirate; appears to have enriched himself by lawful enterprises of various kinds on the sea; has lived in the colonies for a long while. Born in Brittany, he returned and settled there about thirty years since, accompanied by the late Pierre-Antoine Laroque, his only son, husband of

"2d. Mme. Laroque (Joséphine-Clara), daughter-in-law of the above-mentioned; by origin a Creole; aged forty years; indolent disposition; romantic temperament; certain whimsies: a beautiful nature.

"3d. Mlle. Laroque (Marguerite-Louise), the grand-daughter, daughter, and presumptive heiress of the preceding, aged twenty years; Creole and Bretonne; cherishes certain chimæras; a beautiful nature.

"4th. Mme. Aubry, widow of one Aubry, a stock-broker, who died in Belgium; a second cousin, lives with the family.

"5th. Mlle. Hélouin (Caroline-Gabrielle), aged twenty-six; formerly governess, now companion; cultivated intellect; character doubtful.

"Burn this."

In spite of its reticence, this document was of some service to me. Relieved from the dread of the unknown, I felt that my apprehensions had partly subsided. And if, as M. Laubépin asserted, there were two fine characters in the Château Laroque, it was a higher proportion than one could have expected to find among five inhabitants.

After a drive of two hours the coachman stopped at a gate flanked by two lodges.

I left my heavy luggage there, and went towards the château, carrying a valise in one hand, while I used the other to cut off the heads of the marguerites with my cane. After walking a little distance between rows of large chestnuts I came to a spacious circular garden, emerging into a park a little farther on. Right and left I saw deep vistas opening out between groves already verdant, water flowing under trees, and little white boats laid up in rustic boat-houses.

Facing me was the château, an imposing building in the elegant half-Italian style of the early years of Louis XIII. At the foot of the double perron, and under the lofty windows of the façade stretched a long terrace, which formed a kind of private garden, approached by several broad, low steps. The gay and sumptuous aspect of this place caused me a real disappointment, which was not lessened when, as I drew nearer to the terrace, I heard the noise of young and laughing voices rising above the distant tinkle of a piano. Plainly I had come to an abode of pleasure very different from the old and gloomy donjon of my imaginings. However, the time for reflection had passed. I went quickly up the steps, and suddenly found myself in the midst of a scene, which in any other circumstances I should have thought extremely pretty.

On one of the lawns of the flower-garden half a dozen young girls, linked in couples and laughing at themselves, whirled in a flood of sunshine, while a piano, touched by a skilful hand, sent the rhythms of a riotous waltz through an open window.

But I had scarcely had time to note the animated faces of the dancers, their loosened hair, and large hats flapping on their shoulders. My sudden appearance had been received with a cry of general alarm, succeeded by profound silence. The dancing ceased, and all the band awaited the advance of the stranger in array of battle. But the stranger had come to a halt with signs of evident embarrassment. Though for some time past I had scarcely troubled my head about my social claims, I must confess that at this moment I should gladly have got rid of my hand-bag. But I had to make the best of the situation. As I advanced, hat in hand, towards the double staircase leading to the vestibule of the château the piano ceased abruptly. A large Newfoundland first presented himself at the window, putting his lion-like head on the cross-bar between his two hairy paws; immediately after there appeared a tall young girl, whose somewhat sunburnt face and serious expression were framed in a mass of black and lustrous hair. Her eyes, which I thought extraordinarily large, examined the scene outside with nonchalant curiosity.

"Well, what is the matter?" she asked in a quiet tone.

I made her a low bow, and once more cursing the bag which evidently amused the young ladies, I crossed the perron hastily, and entered the house.

In the hall a gray-haired servant, dressed in black, took my name. A few minutes later I was shown into a large drawing-room hung with yellow silk. There I at once recognised the young lady I had just seen at the window. She was beyond question remarkably beautiful. By the fire-place, where a regular furnace was blazing, a lady of middle age and of marked Creole type of feature, sat buried in a large arm-chair among a mass of eider-down pillows and cushions of all sizes. Within her reach stood an antique tripod surmounted by a *brasero*, to which she frequently held her pale and delicate hands. Near Mme. Laroque sat a lady knitting, whom I recognised at once by her morose and disagreeable expression as the second cousin, the widow of the stock-broker who died in Belgium. Mme. Laroque looked at me as if she were more than surprised, as if she were astounded. She asked my name again.

"I beg your pardon . . . Monsieur . . . ?"

"Odiot, madame."

"Maxime Odiot—the manager, the steward—that M. Laubépin . . . ?"

"Yes, madame."

"You are quite sure?"

I could not help smiling.

"Yes, madame, quite sure."

She glanced quickly at the widow of the stock-broker, and then at the grave young girl, as if to say, "Is it possible?" Then she moved slightly among her cushions, and continued:

"Pray sit down, M. Odiot," she said. "I must thank you very much for placing your talents at our service. We need your help badly, I assure you, for—it cannot be denied—we have the misfortune to be very wealthy."

Seeing the second cousin raise her shoulders at this, Mme. Laroque went on: "Yes, my dear Mme. Aubry, I do say so, and I hold to it. God sent me riches to try me. Most certainly I was born for poverty and privation, for devotion and sacrifice; but I have always been crossed. For instance, I should have loved to have had an invalid husband. M. Laroque was an exceptionally healthy man. That is how my destiny has been and will be marred from beginning to end——"

"Oh, don't talk like that!" said Mme. Aubry dryly. "Poverty would agree with you—a person who can't deny herself a single indulgence or refinement!"

"One moment, my dear madame," returned Mme. Laroque, "I do not believe in useless sacrifices. If I subjected myself to the worst privations, who would be the better for it? Would you be any happier if I shivered with cold from morning till night?"

By an expressive gesture Mme. Aubry signified that she would not be any happier, but that she considered Mme. Laroque's language extremely affected and ridiculous.

"After all," continued Mme. Laroque, "good fortune or ill fortune, what does it matter? As I said, M. Odiot, we are very rich, and little as I may value our wealth, it is my duty to preserve it for my daughter, though the poor child cares no more for it than I. Do you, Marguerite?"

A slight smile broke the curve of Mlle. Marguerite's disdainful lips at this question, and the low arch of her eyebrows contracted momentarily;

then the grave, haughty face subsided into repose again.

"M. Odiot," resumed Mme. Laroque, "you shall be shown the place, which, at M. Laubépin's explicit request, has been reserved for you; but before this I should like you to be introduced to my father-in-law, who will be very much pleased to see you. My dear cousin, will you ring? M. Odiot, I hope that you will give us the pleasure of your company at dinner to-day. Good-bye—for the present."

I was intrusted to the care of a servant, who asked me to wait in a room next to the one I had just left, until he had ascertained M. Laroque's wishes. He had not closed the door of the *salon*, so it was impossible for me not to hear these words spoken by Mme. Laroque with the good-natured irony habitual to her:

"There! Can you understand Laubépin? He talked of a man of a certain age; very simple, very steady, and he sends me a gentleman like that!"

Mlle. Marguerite said something, but so quietly that I could not hear it, much to my regret, I confess. Her mother replied immediately:

"That may be so, my dear, but it is none the less absolutely ridiculous of Laubépin. Do you expect that a man of that kind will go running about ploughed fields in *sabots?* I will wager that man has never worn *sabots;* he doesn't know what they are. Well, it may be a prejudice of mine, dear, but *sabots* seem to me essential to a good bailiff. Marguerite, it has just occurred to me, you might take him to your grandfather."

Mlle. Marguerite entered the room where I was almost directly. She seemed vexed to find me there.

"Pardon me, mademoiselle," I said, "but the servant asked me to wait here."

"Will you be so good as to follow me, sir?"

I followed her. She made me climb a staircase, cross many corridors, and at last brought me to a kind of gallery, where she left me. I amused myself by examining the pictures. They were, for the most part, very ordinary sea pieces painted to glorify the old privateersmen of the Empire. There were several rather murky sea-fights, in which it was very evident that the little brig Aimable, Captain Laroque, twenty-six guns, gave John Bull a great deal of trouble. Then came several full-length portraits of Captain Laroque, which naturally attracted my particular attention. With certain slight variations they all represented a man of gigantic height, wearing a sort of republican uniform with large facings, as luxuriant of locks as Kléber, and looking straight before him with an energetic, glowing, and sombre expression. Altogether not exactly a pleasant sort of man. While I studied this mighty figure, which perfectly realized the general idea of a privateersman and even of a pirate, Mlle. Marguerite asked me to come into the room. I found myself face to face with a shrivelled and decrepit old man, whose eyes showed scarcely a spark of life, and who, as he welcomed me, touched with trembling hand the cap of black silk which covered a skull that shone like ivory.

"Grandfather," said Mlle. Marguerite, raising her voice, "this is M. Odiot."

The poor old privateersman raised himself a little, as he looked at me with a dull and wavering expression.

I sat down at a sign from Mlle. Marguerite, who repeated:

"M. Odiot, the new bailiff, grandfather."

"Ah—good-day, sir," murmured the old man.

An interval of most painful silence followed. Captain Laroque, his body bent in two and his head hanging down, fixed a bewildered look on me. At last, having apparently found a highly interesting subject of conversation, he said in a dull, deep voice:

"M. de Beauchêne is dead!"

I was not provided with a reply to this unexpected communication. I had not the slightest idea who M. de Beauchêne might be; Mlle. Marguerite did not take the trouble to tell me; so I limited the expression of my regret at this unhappy event to a slight exclamation of condolence. But the old captain apparently thought this was not adequate, for the next moment he repeated, in the same mournful voice:

"M. de Beauchêne is dead!"

This persistence increased my embarrassment. I saw Mlle. Marguerite impatiently tapping her foot on the floor. Despair seized me, and, catching at the first phrase that came into my head, I said:

"Yes; and what did he die of?"

I had scarcely asked the question, when an angry look from Mlle. Marguerite told me that I was suspected of irreverent mockery. Though I was not conscious of anything worse than a foolish *gaucherie*, I did all I could to give the conversation a more pleasant character. I spoke of the pictures in the gallery, of the great emotions they must recall, of the respectful interest I felt in contemplating the hero of these glorious scenes. I even went into detail, and instanced with no certain warmth of feeling two or three battles in which I thought the brig Aimable had actually accomplished miracles. While I thus expressed the courteous interest of good breeding, Mlle. Marguerite still, to my surprise, regarded me with manifest dissatisfaction and annoyance.

Her grandfather, however, listened attentively, and I saw that his head was rising little by little. A strange smile lighted up his haggard face and swept away his wrinkles. All at once he rose, and, seizing the arms of his chair, drew himself up to his full height; the glare of battle flashed from the hollow sockets of his eyes, and he shouted in a sonorous voice that made me start:

"Helm to windward! Hard to windward! Larboard fire! Lay to; lay to! Grapple, smart now, we have them! Fire, there above! Sweep them well, sweep the bridge! Now follow me—together—down with the English, down with the cursed Saxon! Hurrah!

With this last cry, which rattled hoarsely in his throat, he sank exhausted into his chair; in vain his grand-daughter sought to aid him. Mlle. Laroque, with a quick imperious gesture, urged me to depart, and I left the room immediately. I found my way as best I could through the labyrinth of corridors and staircases, congratulating myself very much on the talent for *apropos* which I had displayed in my interview with the old captain of the Aimable.

Alain, the gray-haired servant who had received me when I arrived, was waiting for me in the hall to tell me from Mme. Laroque that I should not have time to go to my quarters before dinner, and that it would not be necessary for me to change my dress. As I entered the *salon*, a company of about twenty people were leaving it in order of precedence on their way to the dining-room. This was the first time I had taken part in any social function since the change in my condition. Accustomed to the small distinctions which the etiquette of the drawing-room grants to birth and fortune, I felt keenly the first symptoms of that indifference and contempt to which my new situation must necessarily expose me. Repressing as well as I could this ebullition of false pride, I gave my arm to a young lady, well made and pretty, though rather small. She had kept in the background as the guests passed out, and, as I had guessed, she proved to be the governess, Mlle. Hélouin. The place at table marked as mine was next to hers. While we were taking our seats, Mlle. Marguerite appeared guiding like Antigone the slow and dragging steps of her grandfather. With the air of tranquil majesty peculiar to her, she came and sat down on my right, and the big Newfoundland, who seemed to be the official guardian of this princess, took up his place as sentinel behind her chair. I thought it my duty to express at once my regret at having so maladroitly aroused memories which seemed to have such an unfortunate effect on her grandfather.

"It is for me to apologize," she answered. "I should have warned you never to speak of the English in my grandfather's presence. . . . Do you know Brittany well?"

I said that I had not seen it till to-day, but that I was perfectly delighted to know it, and to show, moreover, that I was worthy so to do, I enlarged in lyric style on the picturesque beauties that had struck me during the journey. Just as I was hoping that this clever flattery would secure me the good graces of the young Bretonne, I was surprised to see her show symptoms of impatience and boredom. Decidedly I was not fortunate with this young lady.

"Good! I see," she said with a singular expression of irony, "that you love all that is beautiful, all that appeals to the soul and the imagination—nature, bloom, heather, rocks, and the fine arts. You will get on wonderfully well with Mlle. Hélouin, who adores all those things. For my part I care nothing about them."

"Then in Heaven's name, mademoiselle, what are the things you love?"

I asked the question in a playful tone. Mlle. Marguerite turned sharply on me, flashed a haughty look at me, and replied curtly:

"I love my dog. Here, Mervyn!"

She thrust her hand fondly into the Newfoundland's thick coat. Standing on his hind legs, he had already stretched his huge head between my plate and Mlle. Marguerite's.

I began to observe this young lady with more interest, and to search for the outward signs of the unimpressionable soul on which she appeared to pride herself.

I had at first supposed that Mlle. Laroque was very tall, but this impression was due to the noble and harmonious character of her beauty. She is really of medium height. The rounded oval of her face and her haughty and well-poised neck are lightly tinged with sombre gold. Her hair, which lies in strong relief upon her forehead, ripples at every movement of her head with bluish reflections. The fine and delicate nostrils seem to have been copied from the divine model of a Roman

Madonna, and cut in living pearl. Under the large, deep, and pensive eyes, the golden sun-burn of the cheeks deepens into an aureole of deeper brown, which looks like the shadow of the eyelashes, or may be a circle seared by the burning glances of her eyes.

It is hard to describe the sovereign sweetness of the smile which animates this lovely face at intervals, and tempers the splendour of the great eyes. Of a surety, the goddess of poetry, of reverie, and of fairy realms might boldly claim the homage of mortals under the form of this child, who loves nothing but her dog. In her rarest creations nature often reserves her most cruel deceptions for us.

After all, it matters little to me. I see plainly that I am to play in the imagination of Mlle. Marguerite a part something like that of a negro, which, as we know, is not an object particularly attractive to Creoles. For my part, I flatter myself that I am quite as proud as Mlle. Marguerite. The most impossible kind of love for me is one which might lay me open to the charge of scheming or self-seeking. But I fancy that I shall not require much moral courage to meet so remote a danger, for Mlle. Marguerite's beauty is of the kind which attracts the contemplation of the artist, rather than any warmer and more human sentiment.

However, at the name of Mervyn, which Mlle. Marguerite had given to her body-guard, Mlle. Hélouin, my left-hand neighbour, plunged boldly into the Arthurian cycle, and was so good as to inform me that Mervyn was the correct name of the celebrated enchanter, whom the vulgar call Merlin. From the Knights of the Round Table she worked back to the days of Cæsar and all the hierarchy of druids, bards, and ovates defiled in tedious procession before me. After them we fell, as a matter of course, from *dolmen* to *menhir* and from *galgal* to *cromlech.*

While I wandered in Celtic forests with Mlle. Hélouin, who wanted only a little more flesh to make quite a respectable druidess, the widow of the stock-broker made the echoes resound with complaints as ceaseless and monotonous as those of a blind beggar: They had forgotten to give her a foot-warmer! They gave her cold soup! They gave her bones without meat! That was how she was treated! Still, she was used to it. Ah, it is sad to be poor, very sad! She wished she were dead.

"Yes, doctor"—she was speaking to her neighbour, who listened to her wailings with slightly ironical interest—"yes, doctor, I am not joking; I do wish I were dead. I am sure it would be a great relief to everybody. Think what it must be—to have been in the position I've been in, to have eaten off silver plate with one's own coat of arms, and now to be reduced to charity, to be the sport of servants! No one knows what I suffer in this house; no one ever will know. The proud suffer without complaining, so I say nothing, doctor, but I think all the more."

"Of course, dear lady," said the doctor, whose name was Desmarets. "Don't say any more. Take a good drink. That will calm you."

"Nothing but death will calm me, doctor."

"Very well, madame, I am ready when you are," said the doctor resolutely.

Towards the centre of the table the attention of the company was monopolized by the careless, caustic, and animated braggadocio of a M. de Bévallan, who seemed to be allowed the latitude of a very intimate friend. He is a very tall man, no longer young, of a type closely akin to that of Francis I.

They listened to him as if he were an oracle, and Mlle. Laroque herself showed as much interest and admiration as she seemed capable of feeling for anything in this world. But, as most of his popular witticisms referred to local anecdotes and parish gossip, I could not adequately appreciate the merits of this Armorican lion.

I had reason, however, to appreciate his courtesy; after dinner he offered me a cigar, and showed me the way to the smoking-room, where he did the honours to three or four extremely young men, who evidently thought him a model of good manners and refined wickedness.

"Well, Bévallan," said one of these young fellows, "you've not given up hopes of the priestess of the sun-god?"

"Never!" replied M. de Bévallan. "I would wait ten months—ten years, if necessary—but I will marry her or no one shall!"

"You're a lucky chap! The governess will help you to be patient."

"Must I cut out your tongue, or cut off your ears, young Arthur?" said M. de Bévallan, going towards him and indicating my presence with a hasty gesture.

A delightful conversational pell-mell then followed, which introduced me to all the horses, all the dogs, and all the ladies of the neighbourhood. It would not be a bad thing for ladies if, for once in their lives, they could hear the kind of conversation which goes on between men in the effusive mood that follows a copious repast. It would show them exactly the delicacy of our manners, and the amount of confidence they are calculated to inspire. I am not in the least prudish, but in my opinion this conversation outran the limits of the freest jesting; it touched on everything, gaily outraged everything, took on a gratuitous tone of universal profanation. My education is, perhaps, incomplete, for it has left me with a certain reserve of reverence, that I think should be maintained even in the wildest extravagances of high spirits.

But we have in the France of to-day our young America, which is not happy unless it can blaspheme a little after drinking; we have the future hopes of the nation, those amiable little ruffians, without father or mother, without God or country, who seem to be the raw products of some heartless and soulless machine, which has accidentally deposited them on this planet not at all to its beautification.

In short, M. de Bévallan, who had appointed himself professor of cynicism to these beardless *roués*, did not please me, nor do I think that I pleased him. I retired very early on the ground of fatigue.

At my request old Alain procured a lantern and guided me across the park to my future quarters. After a few minutes' walk, we crossed a wooden bridge over a stream and found ourselves in front of a massive arched doorway, flanked by two small towers. It was the entrance to the ancient château. A ring of aged oak and pine shut in this feudal fragment, and gave it an air of profound seclusion. It is in this ruin that I am to live. My apartments run above the door from one of the towers to the other, and consist of three rooms very neatly hung with chintz. I am not displeased with this gloomy abode ; it suits my fortunes. As soon as I had got rid of Alain I began to write the account of this eventful day, breaking off occasionally to listen to the gentle murmur of the stream under my window, and to the call of the legendary owl celebrating his doleful loves in the neighbouring woods.

July 1st.

I must now try to pick up the thread of my personal and private life, which for the past two months has been somewhat lost among the daily duties of my post.

The day after my arrival I stayed at home for some hours, studying the ledgers and papers of my predecessor, *le père Hivart*, as they call him here. I lunched at the château, where only a few of last night's guests remained. Mme. Laroque had lived a great deal in Paris before her father-in-law's health condemned her to perpetual rusticity. In her retirement she had kept her taste for the culture, elegance, or frivolity which had centred in the Rue du Bac when Mme. de Staël and her turban held sway. She had also visited most of the large cities of Europe, and had brought away from them an interest in literature far exceeding the ordinary Parisian curiosity and erudition. She read a great many newspapers and reviews, and endeavoured to follow, as far as it was possible at such a distance, the movement of that refined civilization of which museums and new books are the more or less ephemeral fruit and flowers. We were talking at lunch about a new opera, and Mme. Laroque asked M. de Bévallan a question about it which he could not answer, although he professes to be well informed of all that takes place on the Boulevard des Italiens. Mme. Laroque then turned to me with an air that showed how little she expected her man of business to be acquainted with such matters; but it happened, unfortunately, that these were the only "affairs" with which I was familiar. I had heard in Italy this very opera which had just been played in France for the first time. The very reserve of my answers excited Mme. Laroque's curiosity; she questioned me closely, and before long put me in possession of all the enthusiasms, souvenirs, and impressions she had got in her travels. Soon we were discussing the most celebrated theatres and galleries of the Continent like old friends, and when we left the table our conversation was so animated that, to avoid breaking the thread of it, Mme. Laroque almost unconsciously took my arm. We continued our exchange of sympathies in the drawing-room, Mme. Laroque gradually dropping the kindly, patronizing tone which had rather grated on me hitherto.

She confessed that she was possessed by a mania for the theatre, and that she thought of having some theatricals at the château. She asked my advice on the management of this amusement, and I gave her some details of particular plays that I had seen in Paris and St. Petersburg. Then, as I had no intention of abusing her good-nature, I rose quickly, saying that I meant to inaugurate my work at once by examining a large farm about two leagues from the château. This announcement seemed to fill Mme. Laroque with consternation; she looked at me, fidgeted among her cushions, held her hands to the brazier, and at last said in a low voice:

"Oh, what does it matter? You can put it off."

And as I insisted, she replied with comical embarrassment:

"But you cannot; the roads are horrible. . . . You must wait for the fine weather."

"No, madame," I said, smiling, "I will not wait a minute; if I am to be your bailiff I must look after your affairs."

"Madame," said old Alain, who had come in, "M. Odiot could have *le père Hivart's* old gig; it is not on springs, but it's all the more solid for that."

Mme. Laroque darted a withering glance at the miserable Alain for daring to suggest *le père Hivart's* gig to an agent who had been to the Grand Duchess Hélène's theatricals.

"Wouldn't the buggy be able to do it, Alain?" she asked.

"The buggy, madame? Oh, no! I don't believe it could get into the lane, and if it did, it would certainly not come out whole."

I declared that I could walk easily.

"No, no," declared Mme. Laroque; "that's impossible. I couldn't allow it. Let me see . . .

We have half a dozen horses here doing nothing; but perhaps you don't ride?"

"Oh, I ride, but—you really need not—I am going to——"

"Alain, get a horse saddled for M. Odiot. . . . Which do you suggest, Marguerite?"

"Give him Proserpine," whispered M. de Bévallan maliciously.

"Oh, no! not Proserpine," declared Marguerite.

"And why not Proserpine?" I asked.

"Because she'd throw you," said the girl frankly.

"Oh, would she? Really? May I ask, mademoiselle, if you ride her?"

"Yes, I do, but she gives me some trouble."

"Oh, well, perhaps she'll give you less when I've ridden her once or twice! That decides me. Have Proserpine saddled, Alain."

Mlle. Marguerite's dark eyebrows contracted as she sat down with a gesture that disclaimed all responsibility for the catastrophe she foresaw.

"If you want spurs," said M. de Bévallan, who evidently did not mean me to return alive, "I have a pair at your service."

Without appearing to notice Mlle. Marguerite's reproachful look at the obliging gentleman, I accepted his offer. Five minutes later a frantic scuffling announced the approach of Proserpine, who was brought with some difficulty to one of the flights of steps under the private garden. She was a fine half-bred, as black as jet. I at once went down the perron. Some kind people, with M. de Bévallan at their head, followed me to the terrace—from motives of humanity, no doubt—and at the same time the three windows of the *salon* were opened for the use of the women and old men. I would willingly have dispensed with all this publicity, but it could not be helped, and besides, I had very little anxiety about the result of this adventure. I might be a very young land agent, but I was an old horseman. I could scarcely walk when my father put me upon a horse—to my mother's great alarm—and afterward he took the greatest pains to render me his equal in an art in which he excelled. Indeed, he had carried my training to the verge of extravagance, sometimes making me put on the heavy ancestral armour to perform my feats of equitation.

Proserpine allowed me to disentangle the reins, and even to touch her neck without giving the slightest sign of irritation ; but as soon as she felt my foot in the stirrup she shied at once, and sent a volley of kicks above the marble vases on the staircase; then sat comfortably down on her hind-quarters and beat the air with her forefeet. After this she rested, quivering all over. "A bit fidgety to mount," said the groom, with a wink.

"So I see, my good fellow, but I shall astonish her. See," and at the same time I sprang into the saddle without touching the stirrup and got my seat before Proserpine had quite realized what had happened. The instant after we shot at a hard gallop into the chestnut avenue, followed by some clapping of hands, which M. de Bévallan had the grace to start.

That evening I could see, from the way people treated me, that this incident, trifling as it was, had raised me in the public opinion. Some other talents of the same sort, which I owed to my education, helped me to secure the only kind of consideration I wished for—one which respected my personal dignity. Besides, I made it quite evident that I should not abuse the kindness and consideration shown me, by usurping a position incompatible with my humble duties at the château. I shut myself up in my tower as much as I could without being boorish; in a word, I kept strictly in my place, so that none should be tempted to remind me of it.

A few days after my arrival, during one of the large dinners which at that season were of nearly daily occurrence, I heard the *sous-préfet* of the neighbouring little town, who was sitting next to the lady of the house, ask her who I was. Mme. Laroque, who is rather forgetful, did not remember that I was quite close, and, *nolens volens*, I heard every word of her reply.

"Please, don't ask me," she said. "There's some extraordinary mystery about him. We think he must be a prince in disguise. . . . There are so many who like to see the world in this fashion. This one has every conceivable talent: he rides, plays the piano, draws, and does each to perfection! . . . Between ourselves, my dear *sous-préfet*, I believe he is a very bad steward, but there's no doubt he is a very agreeable man."

The *sous-préfet*—who also is a very agreeable man, or thinks he is, which is just as satisfactory to himself—stroked his fine whiskers with his plump hand and said sweetly that there were enough beautiful eyes in the château to explain many mysteries; that he quite understood the steward's object, and that Love was the legitimate father of Folly, and the proper steward of the Graces. . . . Then, changing his tone abruptly, he added:

"However, madame, if you have the slightest anxiety about this person, I will have him interrogated to-morrow by the head constable."

Mme. Laroque protested against this excess of gallantry. The conversation so far as it concerned me went no further. But I was very much annoyed, not with the *sous-préfet*, who had greatly amused me; but with Mme. Laroque, who seemed to have been more than just to my personal qualities, and not sufficiently convinced of my official abilities.

As it happened, I had to renew the lease of one of the larger farms on the day following. The business had to be transacted with a very astute old peasant, but, nevertheless, I held my own with him, thanks to a judicious combination of legal phraseology and diplomatic reserve. When we had agreed on the details, the farmer quietly placed three *rouleaux* of gold on my desk. Though I did not understand this payment, as there was nothing due, I refrained from showing any surprise. By some indirect questions, which I asked as I unfolded the packets, I ascertained that this sum was the earnest-money of the bargain; or, in other words, a sort of bonus which the farmers present to the landlord when their leases are renewed.

I had not thought of claiming this, as I had not found it mentioned in the leases drawn up by my able predecessor, which had been my models. For the moment I drew no conclusions from his silence on this point, but when I handed over the windfall to Mme. Laroque her surprise astonished me.

"And what is this?" she said.

I explained the nature of the payment, and had to repeat my explanation.

"And is it a usual custom?" she continued.

"Yes, madame, whenever a lease is renewed."

"But, to my knowledge, there have been ten leases renewed in the last thirty years. . . . How is it we never heard of such a custom?"

"I cannot say, madame."

Mme. Laroque fell into an abyss of reflections, in which, perhaps, she encountered the venerable shade of *le père Hivart*. At length she slightly shrugged her shoulders, looked at me, then at the gold, then again at me, and seemed to hesitate. At last, leaning back in her chair, sighing deeply, and speaking with a simplicity which I greatly appreciated, she said:

"Very well, monsieur. Thank you."

Mme. Laroque had the good taste not to compliment me on this instance of ordinary honesty; but, none the less, she conceived a great idea of her steward's ability and virtues. A few days later I had a proof of this. Her daughter was reading an account of a voyage to the pole to her, in which an extraordinary bird is mentioned—"*qui ne vole pas.*" *

"Like my steward," she said.

I sincerely believe that from this time my devotion to the work I had undertaken gave me a claim to a more positive commendation. Soon afterward, when I went to see my sister in Paris, M. Laubépin thanked me warmly for having so creditably redeemed the pledges he had given on my behalf.

"Courage, Maxime," he said. "We shall give Hélène her dowry. The poor child will not have noticed anything unusual, and you, my friend, will have nothing to regret. Believe me, you possess what in this world comes nearest to happiness, and I am sure you will always possess it, thank Heaven! It is a peaceful conscience and the manly serenity of a soul devoted to duty."

The old man is right, of course. I am at peace, but I cannot say that I am happy. My soul is not yet ripe for the austere delights of

* "Which does not *fly*." But the French verb *voler* is also to *steal*; hence the application.

sacrifice; it has its outbursts of youthfulness and of despair. My life is no longer my own: it is devoted and consecrated to a weaker, dearer life; it has no future: it is imprisoned in a cloister that will never be opened. My heart must not beat, my brain must not think, save for another. So be it! May Hélène be happy! Years are stealing upon me. May they come quickly! I pray that they will; the coldness that comes with them will strengthen my courage.

Besides, I cannot complain of a situation which has, in fact, fallen agreeably short of my worst forebodings, and has even surpassed my brightest expectations. My work, my frequent journeys into the neighbouring departments, and my love of solitude, often keep me away from the château, where I particularly avoid all the more festive gatherings. And perhaps it is because I go to them so seldom that I am welcomed so kindly. Mme. Laroque, in particular, shows a real affection for me; she makes me the confidant of her curious and perfectly sincere fancies about poverty, sacrifice, and poetic abnegation, which form such an amusing contrast to the chilly Creole's multitudinous contrivances for comfort.

Sometimes she envies the gipsies carrying their children on a wretched cart along the roads, and cooking their food under hedges; sometimes it is the Sisters of Charity; sometimes the *cantinières*, whose heroic work she longs to share.

And she never ceases to lament the late M. Laroque's admirable health, which prevented his wife from showing that nature had meant her for a sick-nurse. Nevertheless, she has lately had fixed to her chair a kind of niche like a sentry-box, as a protection from draughts. The other morning I found her triumphantly installed in this kiosk, where she really awaits her martyrdom in considerable comfort.

I have scarcely less reason to be satisfied with the other inhabitants of the château. Mlle. Marguerite, who is always plunged like a Nubian sphinx in some mysterious vision, nevertheless condescends to treat me to my favourite airs with the utmost good-nature. She has a fine contralto voice, which she uses with perfect art, but at the same time with an indifference and coldness which I think must be deliberate. Sometimes, in an unguarded moment, I have heard her tones become impassioned, but almost immediately she has returned to an icy correctness, as if ashamed of the lapse from her character or from her rôle.

A few games of piquet with M. Laroque,

which I had the tact to lose, won me the favour of the poor old man. Sometimes I find his dim and feeble gaze fixed on me with strange intentness, as if some dream of the past, some fanciful resemblance, had half revived among the mists of an exhausted memory, in which the images of a century hover confusedly.

They actually wanted to return me the money I lost to him. Mme. Aubry, who usually plays with the old captain, accepts these restitutions without scruple; but this does not prevent her from winning pretty frequently, on which occasions she has furious encounters with the old corsair. M. Laubépin was lenient when he described this lady merely as embittered. I have no liking for her, but, out of consideration for the others, I have made an effort to gain her goodwill, and have succeeded in doing so by listening patiently first to her lamentations over her present position, and then to her impressive description of her former grandeur, her silver, her furniture, her lace, and her gloves.

It must be confessed that I have come to the right school to learn to despise the advantages I have lost. Every one here by their attitude and language eloquently exhorts me to the contempt of riches. Firstly, Mme. Aubry, who might be aptly compared to those shameless gluttons whose greediness takes away one's appetite, and who disgust one with the dishes they praise; the old man, perishing as sadly among his millions as Job on his dunghill; the good woman, romantic and *blasé*, who in the midst of her inopportune prosperity dreams of the forbidden fruit of suffering; and lastly, the haughty Marguerite, who wears like a crown of thorns the diadem of beauty and opulence which Heaven has forced on her brow. A strange girl!

Nearly every fine morning I see her ride past the windows of my belfry; she bows gravely to me, the black plume of her felt riding hat dipping and waving in the wind; and then she slowly disappears along the shaded path that runs through the ruins of the ancient château. Sometimes old Alain follows her, and sometimes her only companion is the huge and faithful Mervyn, who strides at the side of his beautiful mistress like a pensive bear. So attended, she covers all the country round on her errands of charity. She does not need a protector, for there is not a cottage within six leagues where she is not known and worshipped as the goddess of good works. The poor people call her "Mademoiselle," as if they were speaking of one of those daughters of kings who give poetry to their legends, and whose beauty and power and mystery they recognise in her.

I, meanwhile, am seeking the key to the sombre preoccupation that clouds her brow, the haughty and defiant severity of her eyes, the cold bitterness of her tongue. I ask myself if these are the natural traits of a strange and complex character, or the symptoms of some secret suffering, remorse, or fear, or love, which preys on this noble heart. However slightly one may be interested in the question, it is impossible not to feel a certain curiosity about a person so remarkable. Last night, while old Alain, with whom I am a favourite, was serving my solitary repast, I said:

"Well, Alain, it's been a lovely day. Have you been riding?"

"Yes, sir, this morning, with mademoiselle."

"Oh, indeed!"

"You must have seen us go by, sir."

"Very likely. I sometimes do see you pass. You look well on horseback, Alain."

"You're very kind, sir. But mademoiselle looks better than I do."

"She is a very beautiful young lady."

"You're right, sir, and she's fair inside as well as outside. Just like her mother. I'll tell you something, sir. You know, perhaps, that this property belonged to the last Comte de Castennec, whom I had the honour of serving. When the Laroques bought the château I must own that I was rather upset, and not inclined to stay with the new people. I had been brought up to respect the nobility, and it went against my feelings to live with people of no birth. You may have noticed, sir, that I am glad to wait upon you; that is because I think you look like a gentleman. Are you quite sure you don't belong to the nobility, sir?"

"Quite sure, my poor Alain."

"Well, it's of no consequence, sir, and this is what I wanted to tell you," said Alain, with a graceful inclination. "In the service of these ladies I have learned that nobility of the heart is as good as the other, more especially that of the Comte de Castennec, who had a weakness for beating his servants. Still, sir, it's a great pity mademoiselle cannot marry a gentleman with a fine old name. Then she would be perfect."

"But, Alain, it seems to me that it only depends on herself."

"If you refer to M. de Bévallan, sir, it certainly does, for he asked for her more than six months ago. Madame was not opposed to the marriage, and, in fact, after the Laroques, M. de Bévallan is the richest man hereabouts; but mademoiselle, though she didn't positively refuse, wanted time to think the matter over."

"But if she loves M. de Bévallan, and can marry him whenever she likes, why is she always so sad and thoughtful?"

"It's very true, sir, that mademoiselle has changed a good deal in the last two or three years. Before that she was as merry as a bird; now she seems to have something on her mind, but, if I may say so, it is not love for this gentleman."

"You don't seem very fond of M. de Bévallan yourself, Alain. But his family is excellent."

"That does not prevent him from being a bad lot, sir, always running after the country girls, and for no good either. And if you used your eyes, sir, you might see that he is quite ready to play the sultan here in the château itself while he's waiting for something better."

After a significant pause Alain went on.

"Pity you haven't a hundred thousand francs a year, sir."

"And why, Alain?"

"Because . . ." and Alain shook his head thoughtfully.

July 25th.

During the past month I have made one friend and two enemies. The enemies are Mlle. Marguerite and Mlle. Hélouin. The friend is a maiden lady of eighty-eight. Scarcely a compensation! I will first make up my account with Mlle. Hélouin, an ungrateful young lady. What she considers my offences should rather have secured her esteem. But she is one of the many women who do not care either to give, or to inspire, such a commonplace sentiment. From the first I had been inclined to establish friendly relations with her. The governess and the steward were on a similar footing; we had a common ground in our subordinate position at the château. I have always tried to show to ladies in her position the consideration which seems to me due to those in circumstances so precarious, humiliating, and hopeless. Besides, Mlle. Hélouin is pretty, intelligent, and accomplished, though she rather deducts from these qualities by the exaggerated liveliness of manner, the feverish coquetry, and the tinge of pedantry which are the failings of her profession.

I do not claim any credit for my chivalrous attitude towards her. It seemed to me a sort of duty when, as various hints had warned me, I became aware that a devouring lion in the semblance of King Francis I was prowling round my young *protégée.* This duplicity, which did credit to M. de Bévallan's audacity, was carried on, under cover of a friendly interest, with an astuteness and confidence well calculated to deceive the careless and unsuspecting. Mme. Laroque and her daughter, especially, are too little acquainted with the wickedness of this world, and too little in touch with realities to have the slightest suspicion. For my own part, I was angry with this insatiable lady-killer, and did my best to spoil his plans. More than once I secured the attention he desired to monopolize; and I tried more especially to counteract or diminish the bitter sense of neglect and isolation, which makes women in Mlle. Hélouin's position ready to accept the kind of consolation which was being offered to her. Have I ever throughout this ill-advised contest outstepped the delicate limits of brotherly protection? I think not. The very words of the brief dialogue which has suddenly altered the character of our relations bear witness to my discretion. One evening last week we were taking the air on the terrace. During the day I had had occasion to show some kindly attention to Mlle. Hélouin, and she now took my arm and said, as she bit at an orange-blossom with her small white teeth:

"M. Maxime, you are very good to me."

Her voice was a little unsteady.

"I hope so, mademoiselle."

"You are a true friend."

"Yes, indeed."

"But what kind of a friend?"

"A true friend, as you say."

"A friend who—loves me?"

"Surely."

"Much?"

"Most decidedly."

"Passionately?"

"No."

At this word, which I uttered very clearly and with a steady look, Mlle. Hélouin flung the orange-blossom away and dropped my arm. Since this unlucky hour I have been treated with a contempt I do not deserve, and I should have been convinced that friendship between man and woman is a mere illusion, if I had not had on the following day something like an antithesis to this adventure.

I had gone to spend the evening at the château, and as the two or three families who had been staying there for the last fortnight had left in the morning, I met only the *habitués*—the curé, the tax-collector, Dr. Desmarets, and General de Saint-Cast and his wife, who, like the doctor, lived at the neighbouring little town.

When I came in, Mme. de Saint-Cast, who had apparently brought her husband a handsome fortune, was in close conversation with Mme. Aubry. As usual, these ladies were in perfect agreement. In language in which distinction of form rivalled elevation of thought, they, like two shepherds in an eclogue, alternately lauded the incomparable charms of wealth.

"You are perfectly right, madame," said Mme. Aubry. "There is only one thing in the world worth having, and that is money. When I had money I utterly despised every one who had not, and now I think it quite natural for people to despise me, and I don't complain if they do."

"No one despises you on that account, madame," replied Mme. de Saint-Cast, "most certainly not; but all the same there's a very great difference between poverty and riches, I must confess, as the general knows well enough. Why, he had absolutely nothing when I married him—except his sword—and one doesn't get fat on a sword, does one, madame?"

"No, no, indeed, madame!" exclaimed Mme.

Aubry, delighted with this bold metaphor. "Honour and glory are all very well in novels, but a nice carriage is much better in practice, isn't it, madame?"

"Of course it is, madame; and that's just what I was saying to the general this morning as we came here. Isn't it, general?"

"Eh, what?" growled the general, who was playing cards in a corner with the old corsair.

"You hadn't a penny when I married you, general, had you?" continued Mme. de Saint-Cast. "You won't think of denying that, I suppose."

"We've heard it often enough, I should say," growled the general.

"That doesn't alter the fact that if it hadn't been for me, general, you'd have had to travel on foot, and that wouldn't have been a fine thing for you with your wounds. Your half-pay of six or seven hundred francs wouldn't have kept a carriage for you, my friend. I was saying this to him to-day *apropos* of our new carriage, which is as easy as an arm-chair. Of course I paid a good price for it; it's four thousand francs out of my pocket, madame."

"I can well believe it, madame. My best carriage cost me fully five thousand, including the tiger-skin mat, which was worth five hundred francs alone."

"Yes," replied Mme. de Saint-Cast; "but I have had to be a little careful, for I've just been getting new drawing-room furniture; the carpet and curtains alone cost me fifteen thousand francs. You'll say it's too good for a country hole like this. You're right. But the whole town is lost in admiration, and, after all, one does like to be respected, madame!"

"Of course, madame," replied Mme. Aubry, "we like to be respected, and we are respected according to the money we have. For my part, I console myself for not being respected now, by remembering that if I were as well off as I once was, I should see all the people who despise me at my feet again."

"Except me, by God!" cried Dr. Desmarets, jumping up. "You might have a hundred millions a year, and I give you my word of honour you wouldn't see me at your feet! And now I'll go and get some air, for, devil take me, if one can breathe here!"

So saying, the honest doctor left the room, and my heart went out to him for the outburst that had relieved my own sense of disgust and indignation.

Although M. Desmarets was received at the house as a Chrysostom to whom great license of speech was allowed, his language had been so forcible that it had produced a certain embarrassment in the company, and an awkward silence ensued. Mme. Laroque broke it adroitly by asking her daughter whether it was eight o'clock.

"It can't be, mother," replied Mlle. Marguerite, "for Mlle. de Porhoët has not come yet."

The minute after, as the clock struck, the door opened, and Mlle. Jocelynde de Porhoët-Gaël entered the room, with astronomical punctuality, on the arm of Dr. Desmarets.

Mlle. de Porhoët-Gaël, who had this year seen her eighty-eighth spring, and whose appearance suggested a tall reed wrapped in silk, is the last scion of a noble race, whose earliest ancestors must be sought among the legendary kings of ancient Armorica. Of this house, however, there is no authentic record in history until the twelfth century, when Juthaïl, son of Conan le Tort, who belonged to the younger branch of the reigning family of Brittany, is mentioned. Some drops of the Porhoët blood have mingled with that of the most illustrious veins of France—those of the Rohans, the Lusignans, the Penthièvres, and these *grands seigneurs* had admitted that it was not the least pure of their blood. I remember that when in a fit of youthful vanity I studied the alliances of my family, I noticed the strange name of Porhoët, and that my father, who was very learned in such matters, spoke highly in its praise. Mlle. de Porhoët, who is now the sole bearer of the name, had always refused to marry, because she wished to preserve as long as possible in the firmament of the French nobility the constellation of those magic syllables, Porhoët-Gaël. It happened one day that the origin of the house of Bourbon was referred to in her presence.

"The Bourbons," said Mlle. de Porhoët, sticking her knitting-needle into her blond peruke, "the Bourbons are a good family, but" (with an air of modesty) "there are better."

However, it is impossible not to render homage to this august old lady, who bears with surprising dignity the heavy and triple majesty of birth, age, and misfortune. A wretched lawsuit in some foreign country which she has persisted in carrying on for fifteen years, has gradually reduced a fortune, which was but small to begin with; and now she has scarcely a thousand francs a year. Privation has not broken her pride or embittered her temper. She is gay, good-humoured, and courteous. She lives, no one quite knows how, in her small house with her little servant, and contrives even to find money for charity. To their great honour, Mme. Laroque and her daughter are devoted to their poor and noble neighbour. At their house she is treated with a respectful attention which amazes Mme. Aubry. I have often seen Mlle. Marguerite leave the gayest dance to make a fourth for Mlle. de Porhoët's rubber, for the world would come to an end if Mlle. de Porhoët's whist (halfpenny points) was omitted for a single day. I am one of the old lady's favourite partners, and on this particular evening soon found myself, with the curé and the doctor, seated at the whist-table with the descendant of Conan le Tort.

I ought to mention here that at the commencement of the last century a grand-uncle of Mlle. de Porhoët, who held an office in the establishment of the Duke d'Anjou, crossed the Pyrenees in the suite of the young prince, who became Philip V, settled in Spain, and prospered there. His posterity became extinct about fifteen years ago, and Mlle. de Porhoët, who had never lost sight of her Spanish relatives, at once declared herself heiress to their considerable property. Her claims were contested, only too justly, I fear, by one of the oldest Castilian families allied to the Spanish branch of the Porhoëts.

Hence the lawsuit which the unfortunate octogenarian maintained at great expense, going from court to court with a persistence akin to mania, which her friends deplored and other people ridiculed. Dr. Desmarets, despite his respect for Mlle. de Porhoët, belongs to the party who laughs ; more particularly, because he strongly disapproves of the use to which the poor lady has prospectively devoted her fictitious heritage. She intends to build in the neighbouring town a cathedral in the richest *flamboyant* style, which shall perpetuate the name of the foundress and of a great departed race to all future generations. This cathedral—dream begotten of a dream !—is the harmless hobby of the old lady. She has had the plans made; she spends her days and sometimes her nights brooding on its splendours, altering its arrangements, or adding to its decoration. She speaks of it as already existent: "I was in the nave of my cathedral; to-night I noticed something very ugly in the north aisle of my cathedral ; I have altered the uniform of the *suisse* ;" etc., etc.

"Well, mademoiselle," said the doctor, shuffling the cards, "have you been working at the cathedral since yesterday?"

"Yes, of course I have, doctor; and I've had a rather happy idea. I have replaced the solid wall, which you know separates the choir from the sacristy, by a screen of carved foliage in imitation of the Clisson chapel in the church at Josselin. It is much lighter."

"No doubt; but in the meanwhile what is the news from Spain? Can it be true, as I think I saw in the *Revue des Deux Mondes* this morning, that the young duke of Villa-Hermosa proposes to put an end to the case in a friendly way, by offering to marry you?"

Mademoiselle de Porhoët disdainfully shook the plume of faded ribbons attached to her cap.

"I should refuse absolutely," she said.

"Ah, yes, you say so, mademoiselle! But how about the guitar that's been heard under your windows the last few nights?"

"Bah!"

"Bah? And that Spaniard who has been prowling about the country in a mantle and yellow boots, sighing as if his heart would burst?"

"You are a feather-head, Dr. Desmarets," said Mademoiselle de Porhoët, calmly opening her snuff-box. "Still—as you wish to know—I may say that my man of business wrote to me from Madrid a day or two ago that with a little more patience we should see the end of all our troubles."

"I can quite believe that! Do you know where your man of business comes from, madame? Straight from Gil Blas' cavern. He'll drain you of your last shilling, and then he'll laugh in your face. How much better it would be to give up this folly for good and all, and live at ease quietly! What good will these millions do you? Aren't you happy and respected . . . what more do you want? . . . As for your cathedral, I won't speak of it, because—it is a bad joke."

"My cathedral is not a bad joke to any but bad jokers, Dr. Desmarets; besides, I am defending my rights, I am fighting for justice; the property belongs to me. I have heard my father say so a hundred times, and never, with my consent, shall it go to people who are actually as much strangers to our family as yourself, my friend, or," she added, indicating me, "this gentleman."

I was childish enough to resent this remark, and at once replied: "As far as I am concerned, mademoiselle, you are mistaken; for my family has had the honour of being allied to yours, and *vice versa*."

At this startling announcement Mlle. de Porhoët hastily brought her cards, which she held spread out fanwise, nearer to her pointed chin, and straightening her spare figure, looked me in the face as if she doubted my sanity. By a tremendous effort she recovered her self-possession, and said, as she carried a pinch of Spanish snuff to her thin nose, "Young man, you will have to prove what you say to me."

Ashamed of my foolish boast, and embarrassed by the attention it had aroused, I bowed awkwardly without speaking. Our rubber was played in gloomy silence. It was ten o'clock, and I was preparing to slip off, when Mlle. de Porhoët touched my arm.

"Sir," she said, "will you be so kind as to accompany me to the end of the avenue?"

I bowed again and followed her into the park. The little servant in Breton costume went first, carrying a lantern; then came Mlle. de Porhoët, stiff and silent, carefully holding up her worn silk frock; she had coldly declined the offer of my arm, and I walked humbly at her side, feeling very much dissatisfied with myself. After a few minutes of this funeral march the old lady spoke.

"Well, sir?" she said. "You may speak; I am waiting. You have asserted that your family is allied to mine, and as an alliance of this kind is a piece of history entirely new to me, I shall be greatly obliged if you will enlighten me on the subject."

I had decided that I must at all costs keep the secret of my incognito.

"I venture to hope, mademoiselle, that you won't take a mere joke quite seriously."

"A joke!" exclaimed Mlle. de Porhoët. "A nice subject to joke upon! And, sir, what do you people of to-day call the jokes that can be boldly addressed to an old and defenceless woman, but which you would not dare to utter in the presence of a man?"

"Mademoiselle, you leave me no choice; I must trust to your discretion. I do not know whether the name of Champcey d'Hauterive is familiar to you?"

"I know the Champcey d'Hauterives perfectly well, sir. They are a good, an excellent Dauphin family. What inference am I to make from your question?"

"I am the present representative of that family."

"You!" exclaimed Mlle. de Porhoët, coming to a sudden halt. "You are a Champcey d'Hauterive?"

"Yes, the male representative, mademoiselle."

"That alters the question," she said. "Give me your arm, cousin, and tell me your history."

I thought that in the circumstances it would be better not to conceal anything from her. As I finished the painful story of my family troubles, we found ourselves opposite a small house, remarkably low and narrow. On one side stood a kind of low pigeon-house with a pointed roof.

"Enter, marquis," said the daughter of the kings of Gaël at the threshold of her lowly palace. "I beg that you will enter."

The next moment I stepped into a little *salon* meanly paved with brick; on the faded tapestry of the walls hung portraits of ancestors gorgeous in ducal ermine. Over the mantel-piece sparkled a magnificent clock in tortoise-shell and brass, surmounted by a group representing the chariot of the sun. Some oval-backed arm-chairs and an old spindle-legged couch completed the furniture of the room. Everything shone with cleanliness, and the air was filled with mingled odours of iris, Spanish snuff, and aromatic essences.

"Pray be seated," said the old lady, taking her place on the couch; "pray be seated, my cousin. I call you cousin, though we are not related, and cannot be, as Jeanne de Porhoët and Hugues de Champcey were so ill-advised as to leave no issue.

But, with your permission, I should like to treat you as a cousin when we are alone, if only to make me forget for a moment that I am alone in the world.

"So, cousin, I see how you are situated; the case is a hard one, most assuredly. But I will suggest one or two reflections which have solaced me, and which I think are likely to bring consolation to you.

"In the first place, my dear marquis, I often tell myself that among all the charlatans and ex-lackeys one now sees rolling in carriages, poverty has a peculiar perfume of distinction and good taste. And also I am inclined to believe that God has brought some of us down to a poor and narrow life, that this coarse, materialistic, money-grubbing age may have before it the type of a merit, dignity, and splendour which owes nothing to money, that money cannot buy—that is not for sale. In all probability, my cousin, such is the providential justification of your situation and of mine."

I conveyed to Mlle. de Porhoët my satisfaction at having been chosen with her to give the world the noble example it needs so much, and shows itself so ready to profit by.

"For my own part," she went on, "I am

inured to privation, and I do not feel it much. When, in the course of a life that has been too long, one has seen a father and four brothers, worthy of their father, perish before their time, by sword or bullet; when one has lost, one by one, all the objects of one's affection and worship, one must have a very paltry soul to be much concerned about more or less ample meals and more or less dainty clothing. Certainly, marquis, you may be sure that if my personal comfort only were at stake, I should not trouble about my Spanish millions; but to me it seems but right and proper and exemplary that a house like mine should not disappear without leaving some permanent sign, some striking monument of its grandeur and its faith. And that is why, cousin, I have, in imitation of some of my ancestors, thought of the pious foundation of which you must have heard, and which, while I have life, I shall not relinquish."

Assured of my sympathy, the noble old lady seemed to lose herself in meditation, and as she looked sadly at the fading portraits of her ancestors, only the beat of the hereditary clock broke the silence of midnight in the dim room.

"There will be," Mlle. de Porhoët suddenly resumed, in a solemn voice, "there will be a chapter of regular canons attached to the church. Each day at matins, a mass will be said in the private chapel of my family, for the repose of my soul and the souls of my ancestors. The feet of the celebrant priest will tread a slab of unlettered marble, which will form the step of the altar and cover my ashes."

I bent towards her with evident emotion, with visible respect. Mlle. de Porhoët took my hand and pressed it gently.

"Cousin," she said, "I am not mad, whatever they may say. My father, who was truth itself, always declared that when the direct line of our Spanish branch became exhausted we should be sole heirs to the estate. Unfortunately, his sudden and violent death prevented him from giving us more exact information; but, as I cannot doubt his word, I do not doubt my rights. However," she added, after a little pause, and in accents of touching sadness, "if I am not mad, I am old, and the people in Spain know it. For fifteen years they have dragged me on from one delay to another; they are waiting for my death to finish everything. And . . . they will not have to wait long. Some morning, very soon now, I must make my last sacrifice. My dear cathedral —my only love, which has taken the place of so many broken or suppressed attachments—will have but one stone—that of my tomb."

She was silent; her thin hands wiped away two tears that flowed down her worn face, as, striving to smile, she said:

"Forgive me, cousin, you have enough troubles of your own. Besides, it is late—you must go. You will compromise me!"

Before leaving, I again recommended the greatest discretion in reference to the secret I had intrusted to her. She replied, a little naïvely, that I need not be anxious, and that my peace of mind and dignity were safe in her hands. Nevertheless, during the next few days, I suspected, from Mme. Laroque's increased attentions, that my excellent friend had handed on my confidence. Indeed, Mlle. de Porhoët admitted the fact, declaring that the honour of her family demanded this, and assured me that Mme. Laroque was incapable of betraying a secret intrusted to her, even to her own daughter.

Our interview had filled me with sympathetic respect for the old lady, which I tried to express by my actions. The evening of the next day I taxed all the resources of my pencil in the invention of decorations, internal and external, for her beloved cathedral. The attention seemed to please her very much, and I soon got into the habit of working on the cathedral every evening after our whist, enriching the ideal edifice with a statue, a pulpit, and a rood-loft. Mlle. Marguerite, who seems to feel a kind of adoration for her old neighbour, associated herself with my work of charity by devoting a special album to the Basilica Porhoët, which it is my duty to fill with designs and drawings.

And in addition, I offered my old confidant to take my share in the inquiries and other matters of business connected with her lawsuit. The poor lady confessed that I should do her a service; that though she could still keep up her ordinary correspondence, her sight was too weak to decipher the manuscripts of her archives. Hitherto she had not associated any one with her in this important work, for fear of giving more occasion to the rustic humourists. In short, she accepted me as counsellor and collaborator. Since this, I have conscientiously studied the voluminous documents of her lawsuit, and I have been convinced that the case, which must be sooner or later definitively settled, is absolutely hopeless from the beginning. M. Laubépin agrees with me in this opinion, which as far as possible I have concealed from the old lady.

Meanwhile I have pleased her by going through her family archives piece by piece; she still hopes to find among them some incontestable proof in favour of her claim. Unfortunately, the records are very copious, and fill the pigeon-house from floor to roof. Yesterday I went early to Mlle. de Porhoët's to finish before lunch the examination of packet No. 115, which I had begun overnight. The lady of the house had not risen yet, so, with the help of the little servant, I quietly installed myself in the *salon* and settled down to my dusty work. About an hour later, as I was going joyfully through the last sheet of packet No. 115, Mlle. de Porhoët came in, dragging a huge bundle neatly wrapped up in a white linen cover.

"Good-morning, my dear cousin," she said. "I've heard how you have been working for me this morning, so I determined to work for you. Here is packet No. 116."

I must confess that at this moment Mlle. de Porhoët reminded me of the cruel fairy of folklore, who shuts the princess up in a lonely tower and imposes a succession of extraordinary and impossible tasks on her.

"Last night," she continued, "I dreamed that the key of my Spanish treasure lay in this packet.

So you will very much oblige me by examining it at once. Afterward I hope you will do me the honour to share a frugal repast in the shade of my arbour."

There was no help for it. I obeyed, and I need not say that the wonderful packet No. 116 contained, like its predecessors, nothing more valuable than the dust of centuries. Precisely at noon, the old lady came to offer me her arm and conduct me formally to a little box-bordered garden which, with a bit of adjoining meadow, now constitutes the sole domain of the Porhoëts. The table was set out under an arched bower of foliage, and through the leaves the sunshine of a fine summer's day dappled the spotless, sweet-smelling table-cloth. I had done justice to the chicken, the fresh salad, and the bottle of old Bordeaux, which made up the *menu* of the banquet, when Mlle. de Porhoët, who seemed charmed with my appetite, turned the conversation on to the Laroque family.

"I will own," she said to me, "that I do not care for the old buccaneer. When he first came here he had a large and favourite ape, which he dressed up like a servant, and which he seemed to be able to communicate with perfectly. The animal was a nuisance to the whole country, and only a man without education or decency could have kept it. I agreed when they told me that it was an ape, but, as a fact, I have always believed that it was a negro, more especially as I had always suspected its master of having trafficked in that commodity in Africa. But M. Laroque, the son, was a good sort of man, and quite a gentleman. As to the ladies—I refer, of course, to Mme. Laroque and her daughter, and in no way to the widow Aubry, an extremely common person—as to the ladies, I say, they deserve every good thing one can say of them."

Just then we heard the hoofs of a horse on the path that runs outside the garden wall, and the next moment some one was knocking sharply at a small door near the arbour.

"Yes," said Mlle. de Porhoët. "Who goes there?"

I looked up, and saw a black plume above the top of the wall.

"Open," said a gay voice outside, full of musical intonations. "Open. 'Tis the fortune of France!"

"What? Is it you, my darling?" said the old lady. "Quick, cousin, run!"

As I opened the door Mervyn rushed between my legs, nearly throwing me down. Mlle. Marguerite was tying up her horse to the fence by his reins.

"*Bonjour*, M. Odiot," she said, without showing any surprise at finding me there. Throwing the long folds of her habit over her arm, she entered the garden.

"Welcome this lovely day, my lovely girl!" said Mlle. de Porhoët. "Kiss me, dear. You've been riding too fast, you foolish child. I can tell by your colour and the fire that literally seems to flash from your eyes. What can I offer you, my beauty?"

"Let me see," said Mlle. Marguerite, glancing at the table. "What have you got? Has M. Odiot eaten up everything? Not that it matters. I am thirsty, not hungry."

"I utterly forbid you to drink while you're so hot. But wait a moment; there are some strawberries left in that bed."

"Strawberries! *O giòia!*" sang the girl. "Take one of those fig-leaves, M. Odiot, and come with me. Quick!"

While I chose the largest of the fig-leaves, Mlle. de Porhoët half-closed one eye, and followed her favourite with the other, as she walked proudly along the sunlit alley.

"Look at her, cousin," she whispered, with

an approving smile; "isn't she worthy to be one of us?"

Meanwhile, Mlle. Marguerite, bending over the bed and catching her foot in her train at every step, greeted each strawberry she found with a little cry of delight. I kept near to her, holding out the fig-leaf, in which she put one strawberry for every two she ate, to help her to be patient. When she was satisfied with the harvest we returned in triumph to the arbour. The rest of the strawberries were sprinkled with sugar, and crushed by the prettiest teeth in Brittany with great relish.

"Oh, that's done me good!" exclaimed Mlle. Marguerite, throwing her hat on the seat and leaning back against the side of the bower. "And now, dearest lady, to complete my happiness, you're going to tell me stories of the old days when you were a fair warrior."

Mlle. de Porhoët, smiling and charmed, needed no pressing, and began to tell us some of the most striking events of her famous expeditions with Lescure and La Rochefoucauld. And on this occasion my old friend gave me another proof of her nobility of nature, for she paid her tribute to the heroes of those troublous wars without distinction of party. She spoke of General Hoche, whose prisoner she had been, with almost tender admiration. Mlle. Marguerite listened with an impassioned attention which surprised me. At one moment, half-buried in her leafy niche, her long eyelashes a little lowered, she sat as motionless as a statue; at another, when the story became more exciting, she put her elbows on the table, plunged a beautiful hand into the masses of her loosened hair, and fixed the lightning of her brilliant eyes eagerly on the old *Vendienne*.

Among the sweetest hours of my dull life, I shall always count those I spent watching that noble face, irradiated by the reflections of the glowing sky and the impressions of a valiant heart.

When the story-telling was over, Mlle. Marguerite embraced her old friend, and waking up Mervyn, who was asleep at her feet, declared that she must return to the château. As I was sure it would cause her no embarrassment, I had no hesitation in leaving at the same time. Apart from my personal insignificance in the sight of the rich heiress, Mlle. Laroque was quite at her ease without a chaperon. Her mother had given her the same kind of liberal education she had herself received in one of the British colonies. And we know that the English method accords to women before marriage all that independence which *we* so wisely give them only when the abuse of it becomes irreparable. So we went out of the garden together. I held her stirrup while she mounted, and we set off towards the château.

"Really, M. Odiot," she said, after a few steps, "I am afraid I spoiled your *tête-à-tête* in the garden. You seemed to be very happy."

"Certainly, mademoiselle, but as I had already been there a long time, I forgive you; nay, more, I thank you."

"You are very good to our poor friend. My mother is very grateful to you."

"And your mother's daughter?" I said, laughing.

"Oh, I'm not so easily impressed. I am afraid you will have to wait a little before you get any praises from me. I don't judge people's actions leniently; there is generally more than one explanation of them. I grant that your behaviour towards Mlle. de Porhoët looks very well, but——" she paused, shook her head, and went on in a serious, bitter, and frankly insulting tone, "but I am not at all certain that you are not paying court to her in the hope that she may make you her heir."

I felt myself grow pale. But, seeing how absurd it would be to answer this young girl angrily,

I controlled myself, and replied grandly, "Allow me, mademoiselle, to express my sincere pity for you."

She appeared very much surprised. "Your sincere pity?"

"Yes, mademoiselle, the respectful pity to which I think you have a right."

"Pity!" she said, stopping her horse and slowly turning her disdainful, half-closed eyes towards me. "I am not so fortunate as to understand you."

"It is really quite simple, mademoiselle; if disillusion, doubt, and callousness are the bitterest fruits of long experience, nothing in the world deserves pity so much as a heart withered by mistrust before it has even seen life."

"Sir," said Mlle. Laroque, with a strange vehemence, "you do not know what you are talking about. And," she added more harshly, "you forget to whom you are speaking!"

"That is true, mademoiselle," I answered gently, bowing. "I may have spoken without much knowledge, and perhaps I forgot, to some extent, to whom I was speaking. But you set me the example."

Her eyes fixed on the top of the trees that bordered the road, Mlle. Marguerite asked, with haughty irony:

"Must I beg your pardon?"

"Most certainly, mademoiselle," I replied firmly, "if either of us should ask pardon, it is you. You are rich, I am poor; you can humble yourself. . . . I cannot."

There was silence. Her tightened lips, her quivering nostrils, and the sudden whiteness of her forehead, showed what a struggle was going on within her. Suddenly lowering her whip as if to salute, she said:

"Very well, I beg your pardon."

At the same moment she gave her horse a sharp cut and set off at a gallop, leaving me in the middle of the road.

I have not seen her since.

July 30th.

The calculation of probabilities is never more misleading than when it has to do with the thoughts and feelings of a woman. After the painful scene between Mlle. Marguerite and myself, I had not been very anxious to encounter her. For two days I had not been to the château and I scarcely expected that the resentment I had aroused in this proud nature, would have subsided in this short interval. However, about seven o'clock on the morning of the day before yesterday, when I was working at the open window of my tower, I heard my name called out in a most friendly way by the very person of whom I thought I had made an enemy.

"M. Odiot, are you there?"

I went to the window and saw Mlle. Marguerite standing in the boat that was kept by the bridge. She was holding back the brim of her brown straw hat and looking up at my dark tower.

"Here I am, mademoiselle," I said eagerly.

"Are you coming out?"

After my well-founded apprehension of the last two days, so much condescension made me think, to use the accepted formula, I was the dupe of a disordered fancy.

"I beg your pardon. . . . What did you say?"

"Will you come out for a little with Alain, Mervyn, and me?"

"With pleasure, mademoiselle."

"Very well—bring your album."

I went down quickly and hurried to the bank.

"Ah! ah!" said the girl, laughing, "you're in a good-humour this morning, it seems."

I awkwardly murmured something to the effect that I was always in a good-humour, but Mlle. Marguerite scarcely seemed convinced of the fact. Then I stepped into the boat and sat down at her side.

"Row away, Alain," she said immediately; and old Alain, who prides himself on being a first-rate oarsman, set to work steadily, the long oars moving to and fro at his sides, making him look like a heavy bird trying to fly.

"I was obliged to come and save you from your donjon," said Mlle. Marguerite, "where you have been ailing for two whole days."

"Mademoiselle, I assure you that only consideration for you—respect—fear of . . ."

"Respect! Fear! Oh, dear, no! You were sulking, that is all. We behave much better than you. My mother, for some reason or other, thinks you ought to be treated with special consideration, and has implored me to sacrifice myself on the altar of your pride; so, like an obedient daughter, I sacrifice myself."

I expressed my gratitude frankly and warmly.

"Not to do things by halves," she continued, "I have determined to give you a treat to your taste. So here you have a lovely summer morning, woods and glades with all the proper light effects, birds warbling in the foliage, a mysterious bark gliding on the waves. As this is the sort of thing you like, you ought to be satisfied."

"Mademoiselle, I am charmed."

"Well, that's all right."

For the moment I was fairly contented with my fate. The air was sweet with the scent of the new-mown hay lying in swaths on either bank; the sombre avenues of the park, dotted with patches of sunshine, slipped past us, and from the flower-cups came the happy drone of myriads of insects feasting on the dew. Opposite me, old Alain smiled complacently at me with a protecting look at each stroke of his oars, and closer to me Mlle. Marguerite, dressed in white—contrary to her custom—beautiful and fresh and pure as a periwinkle blossom, shook with one hand the pearls of dew from her veil while she held out the other as a bait for Mervyn, who was swimming after the boat. I should not have wanted much persuasion to go to the end of the world in that little white boat.

As we passed under an arch in the wall that bounds the park the young Creole said to me:

"You do not ask where I am taking you?"

"No, mademoiselle, I do not. It is all the same to me."

"I am taking you into fairyland."

"I thought so, mademoiselle."

"Mlle. Hélouin, more versed in poetic lore than I am, has no doubt told you that the thickets that cover the country for twenty miles round are the remains of the ancient forest of Brouliande, the hunting-ground of those beings of Gaël, ancestors of your friend Mlle. de Porhoët, and the place where Mervyn's ancestor, wizard though he was, came under the magic spells of a damsel called Vivien. Now we shall soon be in the centre of that forest. And if this is not enough to fire your imagination, let me tell you that these woods are full of remains of the mysterious religion of the Celts; they are paved with them. In every shady nook you picture to yourself a white-robed Druid, and in every ray of sunlight the glitter of a golden sickle. The religion of these old bores has left near here, in a solitary and romantic place, a monument before which people subject to ecstasy are usually in raptures. I thought you would like to sketch it, and as it is not easy to find, I will show you the way, on condition that you suppress the explosions of an enthusiasm I cannot share."

"Agreed, mademoiselle, I will control myself."

"Yes, please do."

"I promise. And what is the name of this monument?"

"I call it a heap of big stones, but the antiquaries have more than one name for it. Some call it simply a *dolmen*, others, more pedantic, say it's a *cromlech*, and the country people—I do not know why—call it the *migourdit*." *

Meanwhile we glided gently with the current of the stream between two strips of wet meadow. Here and there, small black cattle with large pointed horns turned and looked fiercely at us. The valley through which the widening river crept, was shut in on both sides by a chain of hills, some covered with dry heather and furze, and some with green brushwood. Sometimes, at the end of a transversal cleft between two hills, we could see the crest of a mountain, blue and round in the distance. In spite of her indifference, Mlle. Marguerite was careful to draw my attention to all the beauties of this austere and peaceful country, and careful also, to qualify each remark with some ironic comment.

For a little while a dull, continuous sound had told us that we were approaching a waterfall. Suddenly the valley narrowed into a wild and lonely gorge. On the left stood a high wall of rock overgrown with moss; oaks and firs mixed with ivy and straggling brushwood rose one above the other in every crevice till they reached the top of the cliff, throwing a mysterious shade on to the

---

* In the wood of Cadoudal (Morbihan).

deeper water at the foot of the rocks. A hundred paces in front of us, the water boiled and foamed, and then disappeared all at once, and the broken line of the stream stood out in a veil of white spray, against a distant background of vague foliage. On our right, the bank opposite to the cliff had only a narrow margin of sloping meadow, fringed with the sombre velvet of the wooded hills.

"Land, Alain," said the young Creole. Alain moored the boat to a willow.

"Now, sir," she said, stepping lightly on to grass, "aren't you overcome? Aren't you troubled, petrified, thunderstruck? You ought to be, for this is supposed to be a very pretty place. I like it because it is always fresh and cool. But follow me through the woods—if you are not too much afraid—and I will show you the famous stones."

Bright, alert, and gay as I had never seen her before, Mlle. Marguerite crossed the fields with a bounding step, and took a path which led along the hills to the forest. Alain and I followed in Indian file. After a few minutes' quick walking our guide stopped and seemed to hesitate, and looked about her for a moment. Then, deliberately separating two interlaced branches, she left the beaten track and plunged into the undergrowth. It was very difficult to make way through the thicket of strong young oaks whose slanting stems and twisted branches were knotted together as closely as Robinson Crusoe's palisade. At least Alain and I, bent double, advanced very slowly, catching our heads against something at every step, and at each of our clumsy movements bringing down a shower of dew upon us. But Mlle. Marguerite, with the greater dexterity and the catlike suppleness of her sex, slipped without any apparent effort through the meshes of the labyrinth, laughing at our sufferings, and carelessly letting the branches spring back after her into our faces. At last we reached a narrow glade on the top of the hill. There, not without emotion, I saw the dark and monstrous table of stone supported by five or six huge blocks half sunk in the earth, forming a cavern full of sacred horror. At first sight this perfect monument of a time almost fabulous, and of a primitive religion, has an aspect of eternal verity and of a real mysterious presence, that takes hold of the imagination, and fills the mind with awe.

The sunshine streaming through the leaves stole through the interstices in the roughly joined blocks, played about the sinister slab, and lent an idyllic charm to this barbarous altar. Even

Mlle. Marguerite seemed pensive and brooding. For my part I entered the cavern, and, after examining the *dolmen* thoroughly, set to work to sketch it. For ten minutes I had been absorbed in this work, forgetting everything that was going on about me, when Mlle. Marguerite suddenly spoke:

"Do you want a Velleda to enliven your picture?"

I looked up. She had wound a wreath of oak-leaves round her forehead and stood at the head of the *dolmen*, leaning lightly against a sheaf of saplings. In the half-light, under the branches, her white dress looked like marble, and her eyes shone with strange fire in the shadow of the oaken crown. She was beautiful, and I think she knew it. I looked at her and found it hard to speak.

"If I am in the way, I'll move," she said.

"Oh, no! please don't."

"Well, make haste; put Mervyn in too. He'll be the Druid and I the Druidess."

I was so lucky—thanks to the vagueness of a sketch—as to reproduce this poetic vision pretty faithfully. Evidently interested, she came and looked at the drawing.

"It isn't bad," she said, laughing, as she threw

her crown away. "You must admit that I am very good to you."

I did. I might even have added, if she had asked me, that she was not without a spice of coquetry. But without that she would not have been a woman. Perfection is detestable, and even goddesses need something besides their deathless beauty to win love.

We went back through the tangled underwood to the path in the wood, and thence returned to the river.

"Before we return," said the young girl, "I want to show you the waterfall, more especially as I am looking forward to a little diversion on my own account. Come, Mervyn, come along, dear dog. Oh, you are lovely!"

We soon reached the bank facing the rocks which blocked the bed of the river. The water fell from a height of many feet into a large and deeply sunk circular basin, which seemed to be shut in on all sides by an amphitheatre of vegetation, broken by dripping rocks. But there were unseen outlets for the overflow of the little lake, and the streams so formed reunited a little lower down.

"It is not exactly a Niagara," said Mlle. Marguerite, raising her voice against the noise of the falling waters, "but I have heard connoisseurs and artists say that it is rather pretty, nevertheless. Have you admired it? Good! Now I hope you'll bestow any enthusiasm you may have left on Mervyn. Here, Mervyn!"

The Newfoundland ran to his mistress, and, trembling with impatience, watched her while she tied some pebbles into her handkerchief. She threw it into the stream a little above the fall, and at the same moment Mervyn fell like a block into the lower basin and struck out swiftly from the edge. The handkerchief followed the current, reached the rocks, danced in an eddy for a minute, and then, shooting like an arrow past the smooth rock, swept in a mass of foam under the eyes of the dog, who seized it dexterously in his mouth, after which Mervyn returned proudly to the bank, where Mlle. Marguerite stood clapping her hands.

This feat was performed several times with great success. At the sixth repetition, either because the dog started too late or because the handkerchief was thrown too soon, Mervyn missed it. The handkerchief, swept on by the eddies from the fall, was carried among some thorny brushwood that overhung the water a little farther on. Mervyn went to fetch it, but we were very much surprised to see him suddenly struggle convulsively, drop his booty, and raise his head towards us, howling pitifully.

"My God! what has happened?" exclaimed Mlle. Marguerite.

"He seems to be caught among the bushes. He'll free himself directly, no doubt."

But soon one had to doubt, and even to despair, of this issue. The network of creepers in which the dog had been caught lay directly below one of the mouths of the sluice, which poured a mass of seething water continuously on Mervyn's head. The poor beast, half-suffocated, ceased to make the slightest effort to release himself, and his plaintive cries sounded more and more like a death-rattle. At this moment Mlle. Marguerite seized my arm, and whispered almost in my ear:

"He is lost. It's no use. . . . Let us go."

I looked at her. Grief, pain, and her violent effort to control herself had distorted her pale features and brought dark circles under her eyes.

"It is impossible," I said, "to get the boat down there; but if you will allow me, I can swim a little, and I'll go and give a hand to the poor fellow."

"No, no; don't attempt it. It's too far. And they say it's very deep and dangerous under the fall."

"You needn't fear, mademoiselle; I am very cautious."

At the same moment I took off my coat and went into the water, taking care to keep a good distance from the fall. It was very deep, and I did not find a footing till I reached the exhausted Mervyn. I do not know whether there had been an islet here which had dwindled and crumbled away, or whether a sudden rising of the river had swept away part of the bank, and deposited the fragments in this place; but, whatever the cause, there was an accumulated and flourishing mass of entangled brushwood and roots under this treacherous water. I got my feet on a trunk from which the bushes seemed to spring, and managed to release Mervyn. Feeling himself free, he recovered at once, and struck out for the bank, leaving me to my fate with all the goodwill imaginable. This was scarcely acting up to the chivalrous reputation of his breed, but Mervyn has lived a long while among men, and I suppose has become a bit of a philosopher. But when I tried to follow him, I found, to my disgust, that, in my turn, I was caught in the nets of the jealous and malignant naiad who reigns in the pool. One of my legs was entangled in the creepers, and I could not free it. It is difficult to exert all one's strength in deep water, and on a bed of sticky mud. And besides, I was half-blinded by the bubbling spray. In short, my situation was becoming awkward. I looked towards the bank; Mlle. Marguerite, holding to Alain's arm, hung over the gulf, and watched me with mortal anxiety. I told myself that it rested with me to be wept for by those bright eyes, and to end a miserable existence in an enviable fashion. Then I shook off such maudlin fancies vigorously, and freed myself by a violent effort. I tied the little handkerchief, now in rags, round my neck, and easily regained the shore.

As I landed, Mlle. Marguerite offered me her hand. It trembled a little, and I was pleased.

"What rashness! You might have been drowned, and for a dog!"

"It was yours," I whispered in the same low tone she had used to me.

This speech seemed to annoy her; she withdrew her hand quickly, and turning to Mervyn, who lay yawning and drying himself in the sun, began to punish him.

"Oh, the stupid! the big stupid!" she said. "What an idiot he is!"

But the water was streaming from my clothes on to the grass. I did not quite know what to do with myself, till Mlle. Marguerite came back, and said very kindly:

"Take the boat, M. Maxime, and get away as fast as you can. You'll keep warm rowing. I will come back with Alain through the wood; it is the shortest way."

I agreed to this arrangement, which was in every way the best. I said farewell, touched her hand for the second time, and got into the boat. To my surprise, when I was dressing at home I found the little handkerchief still round my neck. I had forgotten to restore it to Mlle. Marguerite, who must have given it up for lost, so I shamelessly determined to keep it as the reward of my watery adventure.

I went to the château in the evening. Mlle. Laroque received me with her habitual air of disdainful indolence, sombre preoccupation, and embittered *ennui*, which was in singular contrast with the gracious friendliness and playful vivacity of my companion of the morning.

During dinner, at which M. de Bévallan was present, she spoke of our excursion in a manner that stripped it of all sentiment, and as she went on, said some sharp things about lovers of nature, and finished with an account of Mervyn's misadventure, without mentioning my share in it. If, as I thought, this was meant as a hint of the line I was to take, the young lady had been at needless trouble. However that may be, M. de Bévallan, on hearing the story, nearly deafened us with his cries of despair. What! Mlle. Marguerite had endured such anxiety, the brave Mervyn had been in such danger, and he, Bévallan, had not been there. Cruel fate! He would never get over it. There was nothing for him to do but hang himself, like Crillon.

"Well," said Alain, "if it depended on me to cut him down, I should take my time about it."

The next day did not begin so pleasantly for me as its predecessor. In the morning I received a letter from Madrid, asking me to inform Mlle. de Porhoët that her lawsuit was finally lost. Her agent also informed me that her opponents would not profit by their victory, as the Crown, attracted by the millions at stake, claimed to succeed under the law by which the property escheats to the state.

After careful consideration, I decided that it would be kinder not to let my old friend know of the total destruction of her hopes. I intend, therefore, to secure the assistance of her agent in Spain; he will allege further delays, and on my side I shall continue my researches among the archives, and do my best to preserve the poor soul's cherished delusions to the end. However innocent and legitimate this deception might be, I could not feel at rest until it had been approved by some one whose judgment in such matters I could trust. I went to the château in the afternoon, and made confession to Mme. Laroque, who approved of my plan, and commended me rather more than the occasion warranted. And to my great surprise she finished the interview with these words:

"I must take this opportunity of telling you, M. Odiot, that I am deeply grateful for your devotion to my interests, that each day I appreciate your character more truly, and enjoy your company more thoroughly. I could wish—you must forgive my saying it, as you are scarcely likely to share my wish—I could wish that you could always remain with us . . . and I humbly pray heaven to perform the miracles necessary to bring this about . . . for I know that only miracles can do so."

I did not quite grasp the meaning of this

language, nor could I explain the sudden emotion that shone in the eyes of the excellent lady. I acknowledged her kindness properly, and went away to indulge my melancholy in the fields.

By an accident—not purely fortuitous, I must admit—I found myself, after an hour's walking, in a deserted valley, and on the brink of the pool which had been the scene of my recent prowess. The amphitheatre of rocks and greenery which surrounds the small lake realizes the very ideal of solitude. There you are at the end of the world, in a virgin country, in China—where you will! I lay down among the heather, recalling my expedition of yesterday, one not likely to occur again in the course of the longest life. Already I felt that if such good fortune should come to me a second time, it would not have that charm of surprise, of peacefulness, and—in one word—of innocence. I had to own that this fresh romance of youth, which gave a perfume to my thoughts, could have but one chapter, one page, and that I had read it. Yes, this hour, this hour of love, to call it by its true name, had been royally sweet, because it had not been premeditated, because I had not known what it was till it had gone, because I had had the rapture, and had been spared remorse. Now my conscience was awake. I saw myself on the verge of an impossible, a ridiculous love, and worse, of a culpable passion. Poor and disinherited as I am, it is time to keep a strict watch over myself.

I was addressing these warnings to myself in this solitary place—any other would have served my purpose as well—when the sound of voices interrupted my reflections. I rose, and saw a company of four or five people who had just landed, advancing towards me. First came Mlle. Marguerite leaning on M. de Bévallan's arm; next Mlle. Hélouin and Mme. Aubry, followed by Alain and Mervyn. The sound of their approach had been drowned in the roar of the waterfall; they were only a few yards off; there was no time for retreat, so I had to resign myself to being discovered in the character of the romantic recluse. But my presence did not excite any particular attention, though I saw a shadow of annoyance on Mlle. Marguerite's face, and she returned my bow with marked stiffness.

M. de Bévallan, standing at the verge of the pool, wearied the echoes with the clamour of his conventional admiration. "Delicious! How picturesque! What a feast! The pen of George Sand. . . . The pencil of Salvator Rosa!"

All this was accompanied by violent gestures,

by which he appeared to be snatching from these great artists, the instruments of their genius.

At last he became calmer, and asked to be shown the dangerous channel where Mervyn had nearly been drowned. Again Mlle. Marguerite related the adventure, and again she suppressed the part I had taken in the *dénouement*. With a kind of cruelty, evidently levelled at me, she enlarged on the cleverness, courage, and presence of mind her dog had shown in his trying situation. Apparently she seemed to think that her transient good-humour, and the service I had been so fortunate as to render her, had filled my head with some presumptuous notions, which it was necessary to nip in the bud.

As Mlle. Hélouin and Mme. Aubry particularly wished to see Mervyn repeat his wonderful exploit, his mistress called the Newfoundland, and, as before, threw her handkerchief into the current. But at the signal the brave Mervyn, instead of jumping into the lake, rushed up and down the bank, barking furiously, lashing about with his tail, showing, in fact, the greatest interest in the proceedings, but at the same time an excellent memory. Evidently the head controls the heart in this sagacious beast. In vain Mlle. Marguerite, angry and confused, first tried caresses and then threats to overcome her favourite's obstinacy. Nothing could persuade the intelligent creature to trust himself again in those dangerous waters. After such high-flown announcements, Mervyn's stubborn prudence was really amusing. I had a better right to laugh than any one present, and I did so without compunction. Besides, the merriment soon became general, and in the end Mlle. Marguerite herself joined in, rather half-heartedly.

"And now," she said, "I've lost another handkerchief."

The handkerchief, carried along by the eddies, had naturally landed among the branches of the fatal bush, not far from the further bank.

"Rely upon me, mademoiselle," cried M. de Bévallan. "In ten minutes you shall have your handkerchief, or I shall exist no longer."

At this magnanimous declaration I thought that Mlle. Marguerite looked stealthily at me, as much as to say, "You see, there are others who are devoted to me!" Then she answered M. de Bévallan.

"For Heaven's sake, don't be so foolish! The water is very deep. . . . It is really dangerous."

"It is all the same to me," said M. de Bévallan. "Have you a knife, Alain?"

"A knife?" said Mlle. Marguerite, surprised.

"Yes, a knife. Please allow me . . . I know what I mean to do."

"But what do you mean to do with a knife?"

"I mean to cut a switch," said M. de Bévallan.

The girl looked at him gravely.

"I thought," she murmured, "that you were going to swim for it."

"To swim!" said M. de Bévallan; "excuse me, mademoiselle. . . . Firstly, I am not in swimming costume; next, I must admit that I cannot swim."

"If you cannot swim," she said dryly, "the question of costume is not important."

"You are quite right," said M. de Bévallan, with amusing coolness; "but you are not particularly anxious that I should drown myself, are you? You want your handkerchief, that is the point. When I have got it, you will be satisfied. Isn't that so?"

"Well, go and cut your switch," she said, sitting down resignedly.

M. de Bévallan is not easily disconcerted. He disappeared into the nearest thicket, and soon we heard the branches crack. He came back armed with a long switch from a nut-tree, and proceeded to strip the leaves off.

"Do you think you'll reach the other side with that stick?" asked Mlle. Marguerite, who was beginning to be amused.

"Allow me to manage it my own way. That is all I ask," said the imperturbable gentleman.

We left him alone. He finished his switch, and then set out for the boat. We at last understood that he meant to cross the river in the boat, to land above the waterfall, and to harpoon the handkerchief, which he could easily do from the bank. At this discovery there was an indignant outcry from the ladies, who, as we all know, are extremely fond of dangerous adventures—in which they are not themselves concerned.

"A pretty contrivance, M. de Bévallan. Aren't you ashamed of yourself?"

"Tu-tu, ladies! Remember Columbus and the egg. The idea is everything, you know."

Contrary to our expectation, this apparently harmless expedition was not to be carried through without some emotions, and some risks, for M. de Bévallan, instead of making for the bank immediately opposite the little bay, where the boat had been moored, unluckily decided to land nearer the cataract. He pushed the boat into the middle of the stream and let it drift for a moment, till he saw that as the river approached the fall, its pace increased with alarming rapidity. We appreciated the danger when we saw him put the boat across the current, and begin to row with feverish energy. For a few seconds he struggled with doubtful success. But, little by little, he got nearer to the bank, though the stream still swept him fiercely towards the cataract, which thundered ominously in his ears. He was only a few feet from it, when a supreme effort brought him near enough to the shore to put him out of danger. With a vigorous spring he leaped on to the slope of the bank, sending the boat out among the rocks, where it was at once overturned. It presently floated into the pool keel upward. While the danger lasted, our only feeling was one of keen anxiety, but when it was over, the contrast between the comic *dénouement* and its hero's usual coolness and self-confidence, could not fail to tickle our sense of humour. Besides, laughter is a natural relief when a danger is happily past. Directly we saw that M. de Bévallan was out of the boat, we all gave ourselves up to unrestrained merriment. I should say, that at this moment his bad luck was completed by a truly distressing detail. The bank on which he had jumped sloped sharply and was very wet. His feet had scarcely touched it when he fell backwards. Fortunately there were some strong branches within his reach. He hung on to them desperately, his legs beating the shallow water like two angry oars. As there was no danger, his situation became purely ridiculous, and I suppose that this thought made him struggle so frantically and awkwardly, that his efforts defeated their purpose. He succeeded, however, in raising himself and getting another footing on the slope. Then, all of a sudden, we saw him slide down again, tearing the bushes and brushwood as he went, and renewing his wild pantomime in the water in evident desperation. It was irresistible. Never, I believe, had Mlle. Marguerite been at such an entertainment. She had utterly lost all care for her dignity. Like some mirthful Bacchante, she filled all the grove with bursts of almost convulsive gaiety. Between her shouts of laughter she clapped her hands and called out in a half-suffocated voice :

"Bravo! bravo! M. de Bévallan! Very pretty! Delicious! Picturesque! Salvator Rosa!"

At last M. de Bévallan succeeded in dragging himself to *terra firma*. Then, turning to the ladies, he made them a speech which the noise of the waterfall prevented us from hearing distinctly; but, from his animated gestures, the illustrative movements of his arms, and his air of forced good-humour, we understood that he was giving us a reasoned explanation of his disaster.

"Yes, yes," replied Mlle. Marguerite, continuing to laugh with a woman's implacable barbarity, "it was a great success. I congratulate you!"

When she was a little more serious, she asked me how we should recover the capsized boat, which, by-the-bye, was the best we had. I promised to bring some men the next day, and superintend the rescue. Then we struck across the fields towards the château. M. de Bévallan, not being in swimming costume, could not rejoin us. With a melancholy air he disappeared behind the rocks above the farther bank.

August 20th.

At last this extraordinary girl has revealed the secret of her stormy soul to me. Would that she had preserved it forever!

During the day that followed the scenes I have just described, Mlle. Marguerite, as if ashamed of the impulses of youthful frankness to which she had yielded, wrapped herself more closely than ever in her veil of mournful pride, disdain, and mistrust. In the midst of the noisy pleasures, the *fêtes*, and dances that succeeded one another, she passed like a ghost, indifferent, icy, and sometimes angry.

Her irony vented itself with inconceivable bitterness, sometimes on the purest pleasures of the mind, those that come from contemplation and study, sometimes on the noblest and most sacred sentiments. If an instance of courage or virtue was mentioned in her presence, she examined it minutely in search of its selfish motive; or if by chance one burned the smallest grain of incense on the altar of art, she extinguished it with a disdainful wave of her hand. With her short, abrupt, and terrible laugh, like the mocking of a fallen angel, she seemed determined to blight (wherever she saw a trace of them) the most generous faculties of the human soul—enthusiasm and passion. I noticed that this strange spirit of disparagement took on a special character of persecution—positive hostility—when directed against me. I did not understand, and even now I do not quite understand, why I have attracted these particular attentions. True, I carry in my heart the worship of things ideal and eternal, which only death can tear from me (great God, what would be left me if I had not that!); but I am not given to public ecstasies, and my admiration, like my love, will never be obtrusive. In vain I maintained more scrupulously than ever the modesty which springs from real feeling. I gained nothing by it. The most romantic fancies were attributed to me just for the pleasure of combating them, and perpetually some kind of grotesque harp was thrust into my hands, solely for the amusement of breaking its strings.

Although this open warfare against anything higher than the material interests and sordid realities of life, was not a new trait in Mlle. Marguerite's character, it had been suddenly exaggerated and embittered to the point of wounding the hearts most devoted to this young girl. One day Mlle. de Porhoët, weary of this incessant mocking, said to her in my presence:

"My darling, for some time past you have been possessed by a devil which you would do well to cast out as soon as possible, or you will finish by making up a trio with Mme. Aubry and Mme. de Saint-Cast. For my part, I do not pride myself on being, or ever having been, particularly romantic, but I like to think that there are still some people in the world who are capable of generous sentiments; I believe in disinterestedness, if only in my own, and I even believe in heroism, because I have known heroes. More, I love to hear the little birds singing under my arbour, and I like to build my cathedral in the drifting clouds. All this may sound very ridiculous, my dear, but I venture to remind you that these illusions are the riches of the poor, that M. Odiot and I have no other kind of wealth, and that we are so singular as not to complain."

On another occasion, when I had just received Mlle. Marguerite's sarcasm with my usual impassibility, her mother drew me aside.

"M. Maxime," she said, "my daughter teases you a little, but I hope you will excuse her. You must have noticed that she has changed very much lately."

"Your daughter seems to be more preoccupied than usual."

"And not without good reason; she is about to come to a very serious decision, and at such a moment young girls are apt to be capricious."

I bowed and said nothing.

"You are now a friend of the family," continued Mme. Laroque, "and as such I ask you to give me your opinion of M. de Bévallan."

"I believe, madame, that M. de Bévallan has a very handsome fortune—not so large as yours, but undeniably handsome—about a hundred and fifty thousand francs a year!"

"Yes, but what do you think of him personally, and of his character?"

"M. de Bévallan is what the world calls a perfect gentleman. He has wit; he is considered an honourable man."

"But do you think he will make my daughter happy?"

"I do not think he will make her unhappy. He is not unkind."

"What do you think I ought to do? I am not entirely satisfied with him . . . but he is the only one Marguerite at all cares for . . . and there are so few men with a hundred thousand francs a year. You can understand that my daughter—in her position—has had plenty of offers. For the last two or three years we have been literally besieged. . . . Well, it is time we decided. . . . I am not strong. . . . I may go any day. . . . My daughter would be unprotected. Here is an unexceptionable suitor whom the world will certainly approve—it is my duty to welcome him. Already people say that I have filled my daughter's head with romantic notions—which is not the truth. She has her own ideas. Now, what do you advise me to do?"

"May I ask what is Mlle. de Porhoët's opinion? She is a lady of great judgment and experience, and besides, entirely devoted to you."

"Oh, if I listened to Mlle. de Porhoët I should send M. de Bévallan about his business. But it is all very well for Mlle. de Porhoêt to talk. When he's gone, she won't marry my daughter for me."

"But, madame, from the monetary point of view, M. de Bévallan is certainly a fine match. I do not dispute it for a moment, and if you stand out for a hundred thousand francs a year."

"But, my dear sir, I care no more for a hundred thousand francs than for a hundred pence! However, I am not talking of myself, but of my daughter. Well, I can't let her marry a mason, can I? I should have rather liked to be the wife of a mason, but it does not follow that what would have made me happy would make her so. I ought, in marrying her, to be guided by received opinion, not merely by my own."

"Well, then, madame, if this marriage suits you, and suits your daughter equally well . . ."

"Ah, no! . . . it does not suit me . . . nor does it suit my daughter any better. It is a marriage . . . to speak plainly, it is *un mariage de convenance.*"

"Am I to understand that it is quite settled?"

"No, or I should scarcely ask your advice. If it were, my daughter would be more at ease. Her misgivings disturb her, and then . . ."

Mme. Laroque sank back into the shadow of the hood over her chair and added:

"Have *you* any idea of what is going on in that unfortunate head?"

"None, madame."

She fixed her sparkling eyes on me for a moment, sighed deeply, and said, gently and sadly:

"You may go . . . I won't detain you any longer."

The confidence with which I had just been honoured, had not surprised me much. For some time it had been evident that Mlle. Marguerite reserved for M. de Bévallan whatever sympathy she had left for humanity. But she seemed to show rather a friendly preference than an impassioned tenderness. And I ought to say that the preference was quite intelligible. I have never liked M. de Bévallan, and in these pages I have, in spite of myself, given a caricature rather than a portrait of him, but I admit that he combines most of the qualities and defects that are popular with women. He is absolutely devoid of modesty, which is a great advantage, as women do not like it. He has the cool, mocking, and witty assurance which nothing can daunt, which easily daunts others, and which gives to its possessor a kind of domination and a factitious superiority. His tall figure, his bold features, his skill in athletic exercises, his reputation as a sportsman, give him a manly authority which impresses the timid sex. And he has an air of daring, enterprise, and conquest which attracts and troubles women, and fills their souls with secret ardour. Such advantages, it is true, are, as a rule, chiefly impressive to vulgar natures; but though, as usual, I had at first been tempted to put Mlle. Marguerite's nature on a level with her beauty, she had for some time past seemed to make a positive parade of very mediocre sentiments, and I believed she was capable of yielding without resistance as without enthusiasm, and with the passive coldness of a lifeless imagination, to the charms of a commonplace lady-killer, and, later, to the yoke of a respectable marriage.

All this made it necessary for me to accept the inevitable, and I did so more easily than I should have thought possible a month ago. For I had summoned all my courage to combat the first temptations of a love, equally condemned by good sense and by honour. And she who had unwittingly imposed this combat on me, had also unwittingly powerfully helped me in my resistance. If she could not hide her beauty from me, she also unveiled her soul, and mine had recoiled. Small loss, no doubt, for the young millionaire, but a good thing for me.

Meanwhile I had to go to Paris, partly on Mme. Laroque's business and partly on my own. I returned two days ago, and as I arrived at the château I was told that old M. Laroque had repeatedly asked for me since the morning. I hurried to his apartment. A smile flickered across his withered cheeks as he saw me. He looked at me with an expression of malignant joy and secret triumph; then he said, in his dull, hollow voice:

"M. de Saint-Cast is dead."

This news, which the strange old man had wanted to tell me himself, was correct. On the previous night poor General de Saint-Cast had had a stroke of apoplexy, and an hour later had been snatched from the life of wealth and luxury which he owed to his wife. Directly the news came to the château, Mme. Aubry had started off to her friend, and the two had, as Dr. Desmarets told us, passed the day chanting a sort of litany of original and piquant ideas on the subject of death

—the swiftness with which it strikes its prey, the impossibility of preventing or guarding against it, the futility of regrets, which cannot bring back the departed, the consoling effects of time, etc., etc.

After which they sat down to dinner, and gradually recovered their spirits. "Madame," said Mme. Aubry, "you must eat, you must keep yourself alive. It is our duty and the will of God."

At dessert Mme. de Saint-Cast had a bottle of the poor general's favourite Spanish wine, and begged Mme. Aubry to taste it for his sake. But, as Mme. Aubry firmly refused to be the only one to partake of it, Mme. de Saint-Cast allowed herself to be persuaded that God also wished her to have a glass of Spanish wine and a crust of bread. The general's health was not drunk. Early yesterday morning, Mme. Laroque and her daughter, both in mourning, took their places in the carriage. I accompanied them. About ten o'clock we were at the little town. While I attended the general's funeral, the ladies joined the widow's circle of official sympathizers. After the service I returned to the house, and with some other friends I was introduced into the famous drawing-room, the furniture of which had cost fifteen thousand francs. In the funereal half-light I distinguished the inconsolable Mme. de Saint-Cast sitting on a twelve-hundred-franc sofa, enveloped in crape, the price of which we were told before long. At her side was Mme. Aubry, an image of physical and moral prostration. Half a dozen friends and relatives completed this doleful group. As we took up our positions in line at the farther end of the *salon*, there was a sound of shuffling feet and some cracking of the parquet, then gloomy silence fell again on this mausoleum. Only from time to time a lamentable sigh, faithfully echoed by Mme. Aubry, rose from the sofa.

At last a young man appeared. He had lingered in the street to finish the cigar he had lighted as he left the cemetery. As he slipped discreetly into our ranks Mme. de Saint-Cast perceived him.

"Is that you, Arthur?" she said in a lugubrious voice.

"Yes, aunt," said the young man, advancing in front of the line.

"Well," continued the widow, in the same plaintive drawl, "is it over?"

"Yes, aunt," said Arthur, in curt, deliberate accents. He seemed to be a young man who was perfectly satisfied with himself.

There was a pause, after which Mme. de Saint-

Cast drew from the depths of her expiring soul this new series of questions:

"Did it go off well?"

"Very well, aunt, very well."

"Were there many people?"

"The whole town, aunt, the whole town."

"The military?"

"Yes, aunt, the whole garrison, and the band."

Mme. de Saint-Cast groaned, and added:

"The fire brigade?"

"The fire brigade too, aunt—certainly."

I do not quite see why this last detail should have particularly affected Mme. de Saint-Cast, but she could not resist it. A sudden swoon, accompanied by infantile wailings, summoned all the resources of feminine sensibility to her aid, and gave us the opportunity of slipping away. I was glad of it. I could not bear to see this ridiculous vixen performing her hypocritical mummeries over the tomb of the weak, but good and loyal fellow, whose life she had embittered, and whose end she had probably hastened.

A few moments later, Mme. Laroque asked me to accompany her to the Langoat farm, five or six leagues farther on towards the coast. She intended to dine there with her daughter. The farmer's wife, who had been Mlle. Marguerite's nurse, was ill, and the ladies had for some time meant to give her this proof of their interest in her welfare. We started at two o clock in the afternoon. It was one of the hottest days of this hot summer. Through the open windows of the carriage, the heavy, burning gusts which rose in waves from the parched *lande* under the torrid sky, swept across us.

The conversation suffered from our oppression. Mme. Laroque, who declared that she was in paradise, had at last thrown off her furs and remained sunk in a gentle ecstasy. Mlle. Marguerite fanned herself with Spanish gravity. While we slowly climbed the interminable hills, we saw the calcined rocks swarming with legions of silver-coated lizards, and heard the continuous crackling of the furze opening its ripe pods to the sun.

In the middle of one of our laborious ascents a voice suddenly called out from the side of the road :

" Stop, if you please."

At the same time a big girl with bare legs, holding a distaff in her hand, and wearing the ancient costume and ducal coif of the peasants of this country, leaped quickly across the ditch, knocking over as she came along some of the sheep she was tending. She perched herself with a kind of grace on the carriage-step, and stood before us with her brown, self-possessed, and smiling face framed in the window.

"Pardon, ladies," she said in the quick, melodious tones of her country, "will you be so kind as to read this to me?"

She took from her bodice a letter folded in the ancient fashion.

"Read it, M. Odiot," said Mme. Laroque, laughing, "and read it aloud, if necessary."

It was a love-letter, addressed very carefully to Mlle. Christine Ogadec, ——'s Farm, in the commune of ——, near ——. It was written by an awkward but sincere hand. The date showed that Mlle. Christine had received it two or three weeks ago. Not being able to read, and fearing to trust her secret to the ill-nature of her associates, the poor girl had kept the letter in the hope that some passing stranger, at once good-natured and educated, would interpret the mystery that had been burning in her bosom for more than a fortnight. Her blue, wide-opened eyes were fixed on me with an air of ineffable satisfaction as I laboriously read the sloping lines which conveyed this message:

"Mademoiselle, this is to tell you that my intentions have not changed since the day we spoke on the *lande* after vespers, and that I am anxious about yours. My heart is all yours, mademoiselle, and I wish yours to be all mine; and if it is you may be sure and certain that no one alive is happier on earth or in heaven than your friend—who does not put his name here, but you know quite well who he is, mademoiselle."

"And do you know, Mlle. Christine?" I said, returning the letter.

"Very likely I do," she said, with a smile that showed her white teeth, while she gravely nodded, her young face radiant with happiness. "Thank you, ladies and gentleman!"

She jumped off the step and soon disappeared among the bushes, chanting as she went the deep and joyful notes of some Bretonne ballad.

Mme. Laroque had followed with evident rapture all the details of this pastoral scene, which harmonized deliciously with her favourite fancies. She smiled and dreamed at the vision of this happy, barefooted girl as if she were under a spell. However, when Mlle. Ogadec was out of sight, a strange notion came into Mme. Laroque's head. After all, she thought, it would not have been a bad thing to have given the girl a five-franc piece—in addition to her admiration.

"Call her back, Alain," she cried.

"But, mother, why?" said Mlle. Marguerite

quickly, though so far she had apparently taken no notice of the incident.

"My dear child, perhaps this girl does not thoroughly understand how much I should enjoy, and how much she ought to enjoy, running about barefooted in the dust. It would be nice, at any rate, to leave her some little souvenir."

"Money!" replied Mlle. Marguerite. "Oh, mother, don't! Don't soil her happiness with money."

This delicate sentiment—which, by the way, poor Christine might not have appreciated—was astonishing enough in the mouth of Mlle. Marguerite, who did not, as a rule, pride herself on such subtlety. Indeed, I thought she was joking, though she showed no signs of amusement. However that may be, her mother took the caprice very seriously. It was decided enthusiastically to leave this idyll to innocence and bare feet.

After this pretty episode Mme. Laroque relapsed into her smiling ecstasy, and Mlle. Marguerite fanned herself more seriously than ever. An hour later we reached our destination. Like most of the farms in this country, where the uplands and plateaux are the sterile *lande*, the farm of Langoat lies in the hollow of a valley, with a water-course running through it.

The farmer's wife was better, and at once set to work preparing dinner, the chief elements of which we had been careful to bring with us. It was served on the natural lawn of a meadow, under the shade of an enormous chestnut. Mme. Laroque, though sitting in a most uncomfortable attitude, on one of the cushions from the carriage, seemed perfectly radiant. She said our party reminded her of the groups of reapers we see crowding under the shade of a hedge, whose rustic feasts she had always envied. As for me, I might perhaps at another time have found a singular sweetness in the close and easy intimacy, which an outdoor meal of this kind usually creates among the guests. But, with a painful feeling of constraint, I thrust away an enjoyment that might inflict regret, and the bread of this transient fraternity was bitter in my mouth.

"Have you ever been up there?" said Mme. Laroque to me as we finished dinner. She indicated the top of a lofty hill which commanded the meadow we were in.

"No, madame."

"Oh, but you should go. You get such a lovely view. You must see it . . . Marguerite will take you while they're putting the horses in. Won't you?"

"I, mother? I have only been there once, and it was a long time ago . . . However, I daresay I can find the way. Come, M. Odiot, and be prepared for a stiff climb."

Mlle. Marguerite and I started at once to climb a very steep path which wound along the side of the mountain, passing in some places through clumps of trees. The girl stopped from time to time in her swift and easy ascent to see if I were following her, and, panting a little, smiled at me without speaking. On reaching the bare heath which formed the plateau, I saw, a short way off, a village church, the lines of its little steeple sharply defined against the sky.

"That's where it is," said my young guide, quickening her pace.

Beyond the church was a cemetery shut in by walls. She opened the gate, and made her way with difficulty through the tall grass and trailing brambles, which choked the place of rest, towards a kind of semicircular *perron* which stood at the farther end. Two or three rough steps, defaced by time and rather strangely ornamented with massive balls, led to a narrow platform raised to the level of the wall. A granite cross stood in the centre of the semicircle.

Mlle. Marguerite had scarcely reached the

platform and looked into the space that opened before her, when I saw her place her hand before her eyes as if she were suddenly dazzled. I hastened to join her. The beautiful day, nearing to its end, lighted with its last splendours a scene so vast, so strange, and so sublime, that I shall never forget it.

Facing us, and at a great depth below the platform, extended, farther than we could see, a sort of marsh studded with shining patches, and looking like a region slowly emerging from a deluge. This great bay stretched from under our feet to the heart of the jagged mountains. On the banks of mud and sand which separated the shifting lagoons, a growth of reeds and sea plants tinged with a thousand shades, sombre but distinct, contrasted sharply with the gleaming surfaces of the waters. At each of its rapid strides to the horizon, the sun lit up or darkened some of the many lakes which checkered the half-dried gulf. He seemed to take in turn from his celestial casket the most precious substances,—silver and gold, ruby and diamond—and make them flash on each point of this gorgeous plain. As the planet neared the end of his career, a strip of undulating mist at the farther limit of the marshes, reddened all at once with the glare of a conflagration, and for a moment, kept the radiant transparency of a cloud furrowed by lightning. I was absorbed in the contemplation of a picture so full of divine grandeur, and enriched as with another ray of glory by the great memory of Cæsar, when a low, half-stifled voice murmured:

"Oh, how beautiful it is!"

I had not expected this sympathetic outburst from my companion. I turned eagerly towards her with a surprise that was not lessened, when the emotion in her face, and the slight trembling of her lips, had convinced me of the profound sincerity of her admiration.

"You admit that it is beautiful?" I said to her.

She shook her head; but at the same moment two tears fell slowly from her great eyes. She felt them rolling down her cheeks, made a gesture of annoyance, and then throwing herself suddenly on the granite cross, on the base of which she was standing, she embraced it with both hands, pressed her head close against the stone, and sobbed convulsively.

I did not think it right to say a word that might trouble the course of this sudden emotion, and I turned reverently away. After a moment, seeing her raise her forehead, and hastily replace her loosened hair, I came nearer.

"I am ashamed of myself," she murmured.

"You have more reason to rejoice. Believe me, you must give up trying to destroy the source of those tears; it is holy. Besides, you will never succeed."

"I must," said the girl desperately. "See, it is done! This weakness took me by surprise. I want to hate everything that is good and beautiful."

"In God's name, why?"

"Because I am beautiful, and I can never be loved."

Then, as a long-repressed torrent bursts its barriers at last, she continued, with extraordinary energy:

"It is true."

She put her hand on her heaving bosom.

"God had put into this heart all the qualities that I ridicule, that I blaspheme every hour of the day. But when he condemned me to be rich, he withdrew with one hand all that he had lavished with the other. What is the good of my beauty? What is the good of the devotion, tenderness, and enthusiasm which I feel burning within me? These are not the charms which make so many cowards weary me with their homage. I see it—I know it—I know it too well. And if ever some disinterested, generous, and heroic soul loved me for what I am, and not for what I have . . . I should never know . . . never believe it. Eternal mistrust! That is my sentence—that is my torture. So I have decided . . . I will never love. I will never pour into some vile, worthless, and venal heart the pure passion which is burning in mine. My soul will die virgin in my bosom. Well, I am resigned, but—everything that is beautiful, everything that sets me dreaming, everything that speaks to me of realms forbidden, everything that stirs these vain fires in me—I thrust it away, I hate it, I will have nothing to do with it."

She stopped, trembling; then, in a lower tone, she said:

"Monsieur, I did not seek this opportunity. I have not chosen my words . . . I did not mean to tell you, but I have spoken . . . you know all, and if at any time I have wounded your feelings, I think you will forgive me now."

She held out her hand. When my lips touched that soft hand, still wet with tears, a mortal langour stole through my veins. Marguerite turned her head away, looked into the sombre sky, and then slowly descended the steps.

"Let us go," she said.

Another road, longer, but easier than the steep ascent of the mountain, brought us into the farm-yard. Neither of us spoke a single word the whole way. What could I have said, I who was more to be suspected than any other? I felt that every word from my overcharged heart would separate me still further from this stormy, but adorable soul.

Night had fallen, and hid from every one the signs of our common emotion. We drove away. After telling us again how much she had enjoyed her day, Mme. Laroque gave herself up to dreaming about it. Mlle. Marguerite, invisible and motionless in the deep shadow, seemed also to be sleeping; but when a bend in the road caused a ray of pale light to fall upon her, the fixed and open eyes showed that she was wakeful and silent, beset by the thought that caused her despair. I can scarcely say what I felt. A strange sensation of deep joy and deep bitterness possessed me entirely. I yielded to it as one sometimes yields consciously to a dream the charm of which we are not strong enough to resist.

We reached home about midnight.

I got down at the beginning of the avenue, and took the short way through the park to my quarters. Entering a dim alley, I heard a faint sound of voices and approaching footsteps, and saw vaguely in the darkness two shadowy figures. It was late enough to justify me in stepping into a clump of trees, to watch these nocturnal wanderers. They passed slowly in front of me. I recognised Mlle. Hélouin ; she was leaning on M. de Bévallan's arm. At this moment the sound of the carriage alarmed them ; they shook hands and separated hurriedly, Mlle. Hélouin going towards the château, the other to the woods.

In my own room, fresh from my adventure, I asked myself indignantly whether I was to allow M. de Bévallan to carry on his double love affair uninterrupted, and to let him find a *fiancée* and a mistress in the same house. I am too much a man of my age and time to feel the Puritan's horror of certain weaknesses, and I am not hypocrite enough to affect what I do not feel. But I believe that the morality which is easiest and most indulgent in this respect, still demands some degree of dignity, self-respect, and delicacy. Even in these devious ways a man must walk straight to some extent. The real excuse of love is that it *is* love. But M. de Bévallan's catholic tendernesses exclude all possibility of self-forgetful passion. Such love-affairs are not even sins ; they are something altogether lower in the moral scale; they are but the calculations and the wagers of brutalized horse-dealers.

The various incidents of this evening, combined to convince me, that this man was utterly unworthy of the hand and heart he dared to covet. Such a union would be monstrous. But I saw at once, that I should not be able to prevent it by using the weapons that chance had put into my hands. The best of objects does not justify base methods, and nothing can excuse the informer. This marriage will take place, and heaven will permit one of its noblest creatures to fall into the arms of a cold-hearted libertine. It will permit that profanation. Alas, it allows so many others!

I tried to imagine how this young girl could have chosen this man, by what process of false reasoning she had come to prefer him to all others. I think I have guessed. M. de Bévallan is very rich; he brings a fortune nearly equal to the one he acquires. That is a kind of guarantee; he could do without this additional wealth; he is assumed to be more disinterested than others, because he is better off.

How foolish an argument! What a terrible mistake to estimate people's venality by the amount of their wealth! In nine cases out of ten, opulence increases greed! The most self-seeking are not the poorest!

Was there, then, no hope that Marguerite would see the worthlessness of her choice, no hope that her own heart would give her the counsel I could not suggest? Might not a new, unlooked-for feeling arise in her heart, and, breathing on the vain resolutions of reason, destroy them? Was not this feeling already born, indeed, and had I not received irrefutable proofs of it? The strange caprices, the humiliations, struggles, and tears of which I had been so long the object, or the witness, proclaimed beyond doubt a reason that wavered, not mistress of itself. I had seen enough of life, to know that a scene like that of which chance had this evening made me the confidant, and almost the accomplice, does not, however spontaneous it may seem, occur in an atmosphere of indifference. Such emotions, such shocks, prove that there are two souls already shaken by the same storm, or about to be so shaken.

But if it were true, if she loved me, as too certainly I loved her, I might say of that love what she had said of her beauty: "What is the good of it?" For I could never hope that it would be strong enough to triumph over the eternal mistrust, which is at once the defcct, and quality, of that noble girl. My character, I dare say it, resents the outrage of this mistrust; but my situation, more than that of any other, is calculated to rouse it. What miracle is to bridge the abyss between these suspicions, and the reserve they force upon me?

Finally, granting the miracle, if she offered me the hand for which I would give my life, but for which I will never ask, would our union be happy? Should I not have to fear, early or late, in this restless imagination, the slow awakening of a half-stifled mistrust? Could I, in the midst of wealth not mine, guard myself against misgivings? Could I really be happy in a love that is sullied by being a benefit as well? Our part as the protector of women is so strictly laid upon us by all sentiments of honour, that it cannot, even from the highest motives, be reversed for an instant without casting upon us some shadow of doubt and suspicion. Truly, wealth is not so great an advantage that we cannot find some counterpoise to it. I imagine that a man who brings his wife, in exchange for some bags of gold, a name that he has made illustrious, acknowledged worth, a great position, or the promise of a great future, does not feel that he is under a crushing obligation. But my hands are empty, my future is no better than my present; of all the advantages which the world worships I have only one—my title—and I am determined not to bear it, that it may not be said it was the price of a bargain. I should receive all and give nothing. A king may marry a shepherdess; that is generous and charming, and we congratulate him with good reason; but a shepherd who lets a queen marry him does not cut so fine a figure.

I have spent the night thinking these things over, and seeking a solution that I have not yet found. Perhaps I ought to leave this house and this place at once. Prudence counsels it. This business cannot end well. How often one minute of courage and firmness would spare us a lifetime of regret! I ought at least to be overwhelmed by sadness; I have never had such good reason for melancholy. But I cannot grieve. My brain, distracted and tortured, yet holds a thought which dominates everything, and fills me with more than mortal joy. My soul is as light as a bird of the air. I see—I shall always see—that little cemetery, that distant ocean, that vast horizon, and on that glowing hilltop, that angel of beauty bathed in divine tears! Still, I feel her hand under my lips, her tears in my eyes and in my heart. I love her! Well, to-morrow, if so it must be, I will decide. Till then, for God's sake, let me have a little rest. I have not been overdone with happiness. I may die of this love, but I will live in peace with it for one day at least.

August 26th.

That day, the single day I asked, has not been granted me. My brief weakness has not had long to wait for its punishment, which will be lasting. How could I have forgotten? Moral laws can no more be broken with impunity than physical, and their invariable action constitutes the permanent intervention of what we call Providence in the affairs of this world. A great, though weak man, writing the gospel of a sage with the hand of a quasi-maniac, said of the passions that were at once his misery, his reproach, and his glory:

"All are good while we are their masters; all are bad when we let them enslave us. Nature forbids us to let our attachments exceed our strength; reason forbids us to desire what we cannot obtain; conscience does not forbid us to be tempted, it does forbid us to yield to temptation. It does not rest with us to have or not to have passions, but it does rest with us to control them. All the feelings which we govern are legitimate; all those that govern us are criminal.

Attach your heart only to the beauty that does not perish; limit your desires by your conditions; put your duties before your passions; extend the law of necessity to things moral; learn to lose what may be taken from you; learn to give up everything at the command of virtue!"

Yes, such is the law. I knew it; I have broken it; I am punished. It is right. I had scarcely set foot on my cloud of folly when I was thrown violently off, and now, after five days, I have barely courage to recount the almost ridiculous details of my downfall.

Mme. Laroque and her daughter had gone in the morning to pay another visit to Mme. de Saint-Cast, and to bring back Mme. Aubry. I found Mlle. Hélouin alone at the château. I had brought her quarter's salary; for, though my duties do not, in a general way, trench on the maintenance and internal discipline of the house, the ladies had wished, no doubt from consideration for Mlle. Hélouin and for me, that I should pay both our salaries. The young lady was sitting in the small boudoir near the dining-room. She received me with a pensive sweetness which touched me. For at that moment I felt in myself that fulness of heart which inclines us to confidence and kindness. I quixotically resolved to hold out a helping hand to this poor lonely creature.

"Mademoiselle," I said, abruptly, "you have withdrawn your friendship from me, but my friendship for you remains unaltered. May I give you a proof of it?"

She looked at me and murmured a timid assent.

"Well, my poor child, you are bent on your own ruin."

She rose quickly.

"You saw me in the park that night!" she cried.

"I did."

"My God!"

She came towards me.

"M. Maxime, I swear to you that I am a virtuous girl."

"I believe it, mademoiselle, but I must warn you that in this little romance, perfectly innocent, no doubt, on your side, whatever it may be on the other, you are imperilling your reputation and your peace of mind. I beg you to reflect seriously on this matter, and at the same time I beg to assure you that no one but you will ever hear a word on this subject from me."

I was leaving the room, when she sank on her

knees before a couch, and burst out sobbing, leaning her forehead against my hand, which she had seized. It was not long since I had seen sweeter and nobler tears, but still I was touched.

"Come, my dear young lady," I said; "it is not too late, is it?"

She shook her head decisively.

"Very well, my child. Be brave, and we will save you. What can I do to help you—tell me? Has this man any proof, any letter, I can demand from him on your behalf? Command me as if I were your brother."

She released my hand angrily.

"How hard you are!" she said. "You talk of saving me . . . it is you who are ruining me. After pretending to love me, you repulsed me . . . you have humiliated me and made me desperate. You are the sole cause of what has happened."

"Mademoiselle, you are unjust. I never pretended to love you. I had a sincere affection for you, and I have it still. I admit that your beauty, your wit, and your talents fully entitle you to look for more than fraternal friendship from those who see you every day. But my situation, and my duties to my family preclude my indulging any other feeling for you without being dishonourable. I tell you frankly that I think you are charming, and I assure you that in restricting my sentiments towards you within the limits imposed by loyalty, I have not been without merit. I see nothing humiliating for you in that; what might, indeed, humiliate you, mademoiselle, would be the determined pursuit of a man determined not to marry you."

She gave me an evil look.

"What do you know about it?" she said. "Every man is not a fortune-hunter."

"Oh! mademoiselle, are you a spiteful little person?" I said, very calmly. "If so, I will wish you good-day."

"M. Maxime!" she cried, rushing forward to stop me, "forgive me! have pity on me! Alas! I am so unhappy. Imagine what must be the thoughts of a poor creature like me, who has been given—cruelly—a heart, a soul, a brain . . . and who can only use them to suffer . . . and to hate! What is my life? What is my future? My life is the perception of my poverty, ceaselessly aggravated by the luxury which surrounds me! My future will be to regret, some day, to weep bitterly for even this life—this slave's life, odious as it is! You talk of my youth, my wit, and my talents. Would that I had never had the capacity for anything higher than breaking stones on the road! I should have been happier. My talents! I shall have passed the best part of my life in decking another woman with them, and giving her thereby additional beauty, power—and insolence. And when my best blood has passed into this doll's veins, she will go off on the arm of a happy husband to take her part in the best pleasures of life, while, old, solitary, and deserted, I shall go to die in some hole with the pension of a lady's maid. What have I done to deserve this fate, tell me that? Why should it be mine rather than that of those other women? Because I am not as good as they are? If I am bad, it is because suffering has envenomed me, because injustice has blackened my soul. I was born with a disposition as great as theirs—perhaps greater—to be good and loving and charitable. My God! benefits cost little when you're rich, and kindness is easy when you're happy. If I were in their place, and they in mine, they would hate me . . . as I hate them. . . . We do not love our masters. Ah! this is horrible—what I am saying to you. I know it, and this is the crowning bitterness—I feel my own degradation, I blush for it . . . and I increase it. Alas! now you despise me more than ever . . . you, whom I could have loved so much, if you would have let me; you, who could have given me all that I have lost—hope, peace, goodness, self-respect! Ah! there was a moment when I believed that I was saved . . . when for the first time I dreamed of happiness, of hope, of pride! . . . Poor wretch! . . ."

She had seized both my hands; her head fell on them, and she wept wildly under her long, flowing curls.

"My dear child," I said to her, "I know better than any one the trials and humiliations of your position, but let me tell you that you increase them greatly by nourishing the sentiments you have just expressed. They are hideous, and you will end by deserving all the hardships of your lot. But, after all, your imagination strangely exaggerates those hardships. As for the present, whatever you may say, you are treated like a friend here; as to the future, I see nothing to prevent you from leaving this house on the arm of a happy husband, too. For my part, I shall be grateful for your affection throughout my life; but—I will tell you once more, and finish with the subject forever—I have duties that bind me, and I do not wish, nor am I able, to marry."

She looked at me suddenly.

"Not even Marguerite?" she said.

"I do not see that it is necessary to introduce Mlle. Marguerite's name."

With one hand she threw back the hair which fell over her face, and the other she held out at me with a menacing gesture.

"You love her!" she said in a hoarse voice. "No, you love her money, but you shall not have it!"

"Mademoiselle Hélouin!"

"Ah!" she continued, "you must be a child indeed if you think you can deceive a woman who was fool enough to love you. I see through your manœuvres. Besides, I know who you are. I was not far off when Mlle. de Porhoët conveyed your well-calculated confidence to Mme. Laroque——"

"So you listen at doors, mademoiselle!"

"I care nothing for your insults. . . . Besides, I shall avenge myself, and soon, too. . . . Oh, there's no doubt you're very clever, M. de Chamcey! I congratulate you. Wonderfully well have you played your little part of disinterestedness and reserve, as your friend Laubépin advised you to do when he sent you here. He knew the person you would have to deal with. He knew well enough this girl's absurd mania. And you think you've already got your prey, don't you?

Adorable millions, aren't they? There are queer stories about their origin. But, at any rate, they will serve very well to furbish up your marquisate, and regild your escutcheon. Well, from this moment you can give up that idea . . . for I swear you shall not keep your mask a day longer, and this hand shall tear it from you."

"Mlle. Hélouin, it is quite time we brought this scene to an end; we are verging on melodrama. You have given me an opportunity of forestalling you in tale-bearing and calumniation; but you are perfectly safe. I give you my word of honour that I shall not use those weapons. And, mademoiselle, I am your humble servant."

I left the unhappy girl with a feeling of mingled disgust and pity. I have always thought that the highest organization must, from its very nature, be galled and warped in a situation as equivocal and humiliating as that which Mlle. Hélouin occupies here. But I was not prepared for the abyss of venom that had just opened under my eyes. Most assuredly — when one thinks the matter out—one can scarcely conceive a situation which subjects a human soul to more hateful temptations, or is better calculated to develop and sharpen envy, to arouse the protests of pride, and to exasperate feminine vanity and jealousy. Most of the unhappy girls who are driven to this occupation only escape the troubles Mlle. Hélouin had not been able to guard herself against, either by the moderation of their feeling, or, by the grace of God, through the firmness of their principles. Sometimes I had thought that our misfortunes might make it necessary for my sister to go as governess into some rich family. I swore then that whatever future might be reserved for us, I would rather share the hardest life in the poorest garret with Hélène than let her sit at the poisoned banquets of an opulent and hateful servitude.

Though I had firmly resolved to leave the field free to Mlle. Hélouin, and on no account to engage personally in the recriminations of a degrading contest, I could not regard without misgiving the probable consequences of the treacherous war just declared against me. Evidently, I was threatened where I was most sensitive—in my love and in my honour. Mistress of the secret of my heart, mingling truth and falsehood with the skilful perfidy of her sex, Mlle. Hélouin might easily show my conduct in an unfavourable light, turn all the precautions and scruples of my delicacy against me, and give my simplest actions the appearance of deliberate intrigue. I could not foresee the form her malevolence would take, but I could depend upon her to choose the most effectual methods. Better than any one, she knew the weak places in the imaginations she wished to impress. Over Mlle. Marguerite and her mother she had the advantage which dissimulation usually has over frankness, and cunning over simplicity. They trusted her with the trust that is born of long use and daily association. Her masters, as she called them, were not likely to suspect that under the pretty brightness and obsequious consideration which she assumed with such consummate art she concealed a frenzy of pride and ingratitude which was eating her miserable heart away. It was too probable that a hand so sure and skilful would pour its poison with complete success into hearts thus prepared. It was true Mlle. Hélouin might be afraid that by yielding to her resentment she would thrust Mlle. Marguerite's hand into that of M. de Bévallan, and hasten a marriage which would be the ruin of her own ambition; but I knew that the woman who hates does not calculate, and risks everything. So I awaited from her the swiftest and blindest of vengeance, and I was right.

In painful anxiety I passed the hours that

should have been given to sweeter thoughts. All that a proud spirit finds most galling in dependence, the suspicion hardest for a loyal conscience, the scorn most bitter to a loving heart, I endured in anticipation. Never in my worst hours had adversity offered me a cup so full. However, I tried to work as usual. About five o'clock I went to the château. The ladies had returned during the afternoon. In the drawing-room I found Mlle. Marguerite, Mme. Aubry, M. de Bévallan, and two or three casual guests. Mlle. Marguerite did not appear to be aware of my presence, but continued to talk to M. de Bévallan in a more animated style than usual. They were discussing an impromptu dance, which was to take place the same evening at a neighbouring château. She was going with her mother, and urged M. de Bévallan to accompany them. He excused himself on the ground that he had left his house that morning before receiving the invitation, and that his costume was inadmissible. With an eager and affectionate coquetry which evidently surprised even him, Mlle. Marguerite persisted, saying that there was still time to go back and dress and return to fetch them. She promised that a nice little dinner should be kept for him. M. de Bévallan said that his carriage horses were not available, and that he could not ride back in evening dress.

"Very well," replied Mlle. Marguerite; "they shall drive you over in the dog-cart."

At the same moment she turned towards me for the first time, with a look in which I saw the thunderbolt that was about to fall.

"M. Odiot," she said in a sharp, imperious tone, "go and tell them to put the horse in."

This imperious order was so little in harmony with such as I was accustomed to receive here, or such as I could be expected to tolerate, that the attention and curiosity of the most indifferent were excited.

There was an awkward silence. M. de Bévallan glanced in surprise at Mlle. Marguerite; then he looked at me, and got up with a very serious air. If they thought I should give way to some mad prompting of anger they were mistaken. It was true that the insulting words which had just fallen on me from a mouth so beautiful, so beloved, and so cruel, had struck the icy coldness of death to the very depths of my being. A blade of steel piercing my heart could hardly have caused me keener pain. But never had I been calmer. The bell which Mme. Laroque uses to summon her servants stood on a table within my reach. I touched it with my finger. A man-servant entered almost directly.

"I think," I said to him, "Mlle. Marguerite has some orders to give you."

At this speech, which she had heard in amazement, Marguerite shook her head quickly, and dismissed the man. I longed to get out of this room, where I seemed to be choking, but, in view of M. de Bévallan's provoking manner, I could not withdraw.

"Upon my word," he murmured, "there's something very strange about all this."

I took no notice of him. Mlle. Marguerite said something to him under her breath.

"I obey, mademoiselle," he said in a louder tone; "but you will allow me to express my sincere regret that I have not the right to interpose here."

I rose immediately.

"M. de Bévallan," I said, standing within a pace or two of him, "that regret is quite superfluous, for though I have not thought fit to obey Mlle. Laroque's orders, I am entirely at yours . . . and I shall expect to receive them."

"Very good, very good, sir; nothing could be better," replied M. de Bévallan, waving his hand airily to reassure the ladies.

We bowed to one another and I went out. I dined alone in my tower. Poor Alain waited on me as usual. No doubt he had heard of what had occurred, for he kept looking at me mournfully, sighed often and deeply, and, contrary to his custom, preserved a gloomy silence, only breaking it to reply, in answer to my question, that the ladies had decided not to go to the ball.

After a hurried meal, I put my papers in order and wrote a few words to M. Laubépin. In view of a possible contingency I recommended Hélène to his care. The thought that I might leave her unprotected and friendless nearly broke my heart, without in the least affecting my immovable principles. I may deceive myself, but I have always thought that honour in our modern life is paramount in the hierarchy of duties. It takes the place of so many virtues which have nearly faded from our consciences, of so many dormant beliefs; it plays such a tutelary part in the present state of society, that I would never consent to weaken its claims, or lessen its obligations. In its indefinite character, there is something superior to law and morality: one does not reason about it; one feels it. It is a religion. If we have no longer the folly of the Cross, let us keep the folly of Honour! Moreover, no sentiment has ever taken such deep root in the human soul without the sanction of reason. It is better that a girl or a wife should be alone in the world, than that she should be protected by a dishonoured brother or husband.

Each moment I expected a letter from M. de Bévallan. I was getting ready to go to the collector of taxes in the town, a young officer who had been wounded in the Crimea, and ask him to be my second, when some one knocked at my door. M. de Bévallan himself came in. Apart from a slight shade of embarrassment, his face expressed nothing but a frank and joyful kindliness.

"M. Odiot," he said, as I looked at him in surprise, "this is rather an unusual step, but, thank Heaven, my service-records place my courage beyond suspicion. On the other hand, I have such good reason for feeling happy to-night that I have no room for rancour or enmity. Lastly, I am obeying orders which will now be more sacred to me than ever. In short, I come to offer you my hand."

I bowed gravely and took his hand.

"Now," he went on as he sat down, "I can execute my commission comfortably. A little while ago Mlle. Marguerite, in a thoughtless moment, gave you some instructions which most assuredly did not come within your province. Very properly, your susceptibility was aroused, we quite recognise that, and now the ladies charge me to beg that you will accept their regrets. They would be in despair if the misconception of a moment could deprive them of your good offices, which they value extremely, and put an end to relations which they esteem most highly. Speaking for myself, I have this evening acquired the right to add my entreaties to those of the ladies. Something I have long desired has been granted me, and I shall be personally indebted to you if you will prevent the happy memories of this day from being marred by a separation which would be at once disadvantageous and painful to the family into which I shall shortly enter."

"M. de Bévallan," I said, "I fully recognise and appreciate all that you have said on behalf of the ladies, as well as on your own account. You will excuse me from giving a final answer immediately. This is a matter which requires more judicial consideration than I can give it at present."

"At least," said M. de Bévallan, "you will let me take back a hopeful report. Come, M. Odiot, since we have the opportunity, let us break through the barrier of ice that has kept us apart till now. As far as I am concerned, I am quite willing. In the first place, Mme. Laroque, without revealing a secret that does not belong to her, has given me to understand that under the kind of mystery with which you surround yourself, there are circumstances which reflect the highest credit on you. And, besides, I have a private reason for being grateful to you. I know that you have lately been consulted in reference to my intentions towards Mlle. Laroque, and that I have cause to congratulate myself on your opinion."

"My dear sir, I do not think I deserve——"

"Oh, I know!" he continued, laughing. "You didn't praise me up to the skies, but, at all events, you did me no harm. And I admit that you showed real insight. You said that though Mlle. Marguerite might not be absolutely happy with me, she would not be unhappy. Well, the prophet Daniel could not have spoken better. The truth is, the dear child will never be absolutely happy with any one, because she will not find in the whole world a husband who will talk poetry to her from morning to night. . . . They're not to be had. I am no more capable of it than any one else, I own; but—as you were good enough to say—I am an honourable man. And really, when we know one another better, you will be convinced of it. I am not a brute; I am a good fellow. God knows I have faults . . . one especially: I am fond of pretty women. . . . I am, I can't deny it. But what does it matter? It shows that one has a good heart. Besides, here I am in port . . . and I am delighted, because—between ourselves—I was getting into a bit of a mess. In short, I mean only to think about my wife and children in future. So, like you, I believe Marguerite will be perfectly happy—that is to say, as far as she could be in this world with ideas like hers. For, after all, I shall be good to her; I shall refuse her nothing, and I shall do even more than she desires. But if she asks me for the moon and the stars, I can't go and fetch them to please her . . . that's not possible. . . . And now, my dear friend, your hand once more."

I gave it him. He got up.

"Good! I hope that you will stay with us now. . . . Come, let me see that a brighter face! We will make your life as pleasant as possible, but you'll have to help us a bit, you know. You cultivate your sadness, I fancy. You live, if I may say so, too much like an owl. You're a kind of Spaniard such as one rarely sees. You must drop that sort of thing. You are young and good-looking, you have wit and talents; make the best of those qualities. Listen. Why not try a flirtation with little Hélouin. . . . It would amuse you. She is very charming, and she would suit you. But, deuce take me! I am rather forgetting my promotion to high dignities! . . . And now, good-bye, Maxime, till to-morrow, isn't it?"

"Till to-morrow, certainly."

And this honest gentleman—who is the sort of Spaniard one often sees!—left me to my reflections.

October 1st.

A strange thing has happened. Though the results are not, so far, very satisfactory, they have done me good. The blow I had received had left me numb with grief. This at least makes me feel that I am alive, and for the first time for three long weeks I have had the courage to open this book and take up my pen. Every satisfaction having been given to me, I thought there was no longer any reason for leaving, at least suddenly, a position and advantages which, after all, I need, and could not easily replace. The mere prospect of the personal sufferings I had to face, which, moreover, were the result of my own weakness, could not entitle me to shirk duties which involved other interests than my own. And more; I did not intend that Mlle. Marguerite should interpret my sudden flight as the result of pique at the loss of a good match. I made it a point of honour to show her an unruffled front up to the altar itself. As for my heart—that she could not see. So I contented myself with informing M. Laubépin that certain things incident to my situation might at any moment become unbearable, and that I eagerly desired some less lucrative but more independent occupation.

The next day I appeared at the château, where M. de Bévallan received me cordially. I greeted the ladies with all the self-possession I could command. There was, of course, no explanation. Mme. Laroque seemed moved and thoughtful; Mlle. Marguerite was a little highly strung still, but polite. As for Mlle. Hélouin, she was very pale, and kept her eyes fixed on her work. The poor girl could not have been very much delighted with the final result of her diplomacy. She endeavoured once or twice to dart a look of scorn and menace at M. de Bévallan; but though this stormy atmosphere might have troubled a neophyte, M. de Bévallan breathed, moved, and fluttered about in it entirely at his ease. His regal self-possession evidently irritated Mlle. Hélouin, but it quelled her at the same time. I am sure, however, that she would have played him the same sort of trick she had played me the day before, and with far more excuse, if she had not been afraid of ruining herself as well as her accomplice. But it was most likely that if she yielded to her jealous rage, and admitted her ingratitude and duplicity, she would ruin herself only, and she was quite clever enough to see this. In fact, M. de Bévallan was not the kind of man to have run any risks with her, without having provided himself with some very effective weapon which he would use with pitiless indifference. Of course, Mlle. Hélouin might tell herself that the night before they had believed her when she made other false accusations, but she knew that the falsehood which flatters or wounds is much more readily believed than mere general truth. So she suffered in silence, not, I suppose, without feeling keenly that the sword of treachery sometimes turns against the person who makes use of it. During this day and those which followed I had to bear a kind of torture I had foreseen, though without realizing how painful it would be. The marriage was fixed for a month later. All the preparations had to be made at once and in great haste. Regularly each morning came one of Mme. Prévost's bouquets. Laces, dresses, jewels poured in and were exhibited every evening to interested and envious ladies. I had to give my opinion and my advice on everything. Mlle. Marguerite begged for them with almost cruel persistence. I responded as graciously as I could, and then returned to my tower and took from a secret drawer the tattered handkerchief I had won at the risk of my life, and I dried my tears with it. Weakness again! But what would you have? I love her. Treachery, enmity, hopeless misunderstandings, her pride and mine, separate us forever! So let it be, but nothing can prevent me from living and dying with my heart full of her.

As for M. de Bévallan, I did not hate him; he was not worthy of it. He is a vulgar but harmless soul. Thank God! I could receive the overtures of his shallow friendliness without hypocrisy, and put my hand tranquilly in his. But if he was too insignificant for my resentment, that did not lessen the deep and lacerating agony with which I recognised his unworthiness of the rare creature he would soon possess—and never know. I cannot, and I dare not, describe the flood of bitter thoughts, of nameless sensations which have been aroused in me at the thought of this odious *mé-*

salliance, and have not yet subsided. Love, real true love, has something sacred in it, which gives an almost superhuman character to its pain as to its joy.

To the man who loves her, a woman has a sort of divinity of which no other man knows the secret, which belongs only to her lover, and to see even the threshold of this mystery profaned by another gives us a strange and indescribable shock—a horror, as of sacrilege. It is not merely that a precious possession is taken from you; it is an altar polluted, a mystery violated, a god defiled! This is jealousy. At least, it is mine. In all sincerity it seemed to me that in the whole world I only had eyes to see, intelligence to understand, and a heart to worship in its full perfection the beauty of this angel. With any other she would be cast away, and lost; body and soul, she was destined for me from all eternity. So vast was my pride! I expiated it with suffering as immeasurable.

Nevertheless, some mocking demon whispered that in all probability Marguerite would find more peace and real happiness in the kindly friendship of a judicious husband, than she would have enjoyed in the poetic passion of a romantic lover. Is it true? Is it possible? I do not believe it.

She will have peace! Granted. But peace, after all, is not the best thing in life, nor the highest kind of happiness. If insensibility and a petrified heart sufficed to make us happy, too many people who do not deserve it would be happy. By dint of reasoning and calculation we come to blaspheme against God, and to degrade his work. God gives peace to the dead; to the living he gives passion! Yes, in addition to the vulgar interests of daily life, which I am not so foolish as to expect to set aside, a certain poetry is permitted, nay, enjoined. That is the heritage of the immortal soul. And this soul must feel, and sometimes reveal itself, whether by visions that transcend the real, by aspirations that out-soar the possible, by storms, or by tears. Yes, there is suffering which is better than happiness, or, rather, which is itself happiness—that of a living creature who knows all the agonies of the heart, and all the illusions of the mind, and who accepts these noble torments with an equable mind and a fraternal heart. That is the romance which every one who claims to be a man, and to justify that claim, may, and indeed is bound to put into his life.

And, after all, this boasted peace will not be hers. The marriage of two stolid hearts, of two frozen imaginations, may produce the calm of lifelessness. I can believe that, but the union of life with death cannot be endured without a horrible oppression and ceaseless anguish.

In the midst of these personal miseries, which increased each day in intensity, my only refuge was my poor old friend, Mlle. de Porhoët. She did not know, or pretended not to know, the state of my heart; but with her remote and perhaps involuntary allusions she touched my bleeding wounds with a woman's light and delicate hand. And this soul, the living symbol of sacrifice and resignation, which seemed already to float above our earth, had a detachment, a calmness, and a gentle firmness, which seemed to descend on me. I came to understand her innocent delusion, and to share it with something of the same simplicity. Bent over the album, I wandered with her for hours through the cloisters of her cathedral, and breathed for a while the vague perfumes of an ideal serenity.

I further found at the old lady's house another kind of distraction. Habit gives an interest to every kind of work. To prevent Mlle. de Porhoët from suspecting the final loss of her case, I regularly continued the exploration of the family archives. Among the confused mass I occasionally came across traditions, legends, and traces of old-world customs which awakened my curiosity and carried back my thoughts to far-off days remote from the crushing reality of life. My perseverance maintained Mlle. de Porhoët in her illusions, and she was grateful to me beyond my deserts. For I had come to take an interest in this work—now practically useless—which repaid me for all my trouble, and gave me a wholesome distraction from my grief.

As the fateful day approached, Mlle. Marguerite lost the feverish vivacity which had seemed to inspire her since the date of the marriage had been fixed, and relapsed at times into the fits of indolence and sombre reverie formerly habitual to her. Once or twice I surprised her watching me in wondering perplexity. Mme. Laroque, too, often looked at me with an anxious and hesitating air, as if she wished and yet feared to discuss some painful subject with me. The day before yesterday I found myself by chance alone with her in the *salon*, which Mlle. Hélouin had just left to give some order. The trivial conversation in which we had been engaged ceased suddenly, as by common consent. After a short silence, Mme. Laroque said, in a voice full of emotion :

"M. Odiot, you are not wise in your choice of confidants."

"Confidants, madame? I do not follow you. Except Mlle. de Porhoët, I have had no confidant in this place."

"Alas!" she replied, "I wish to believe you . . . I *do* believe you . . . but that is not enough——"

At this moment Mlle. Hélouin came in, and no more could be said.

The day after—yesterday—I had ridden over in the morning to superintend some wood-cutting in the neighbourhood. I was returning to the château about four in the afternoon, when, at a sharp turn of the road, I found myself face to face with Mlle. Marguerite. She was alone. I prepared to pass her with a bow, but she stopped her horse.

"What a fine autumn day!" she said.

"Yes, mademoiselle. You are going for a ride?"

"As you see. I am making the best of my last moments of independence, and, in fact, I have been rather abusing my liberty, for I am somewhat tired of solitude. But Alain is wanted at the house. . . . Poor Mervyn is lame. . . . You would not care to take his place?"

"With pleasure. Where are you going?"

"Well . . I thought of riding as far as the tower of Elven."

With her whip she indicated the misty summit of a hill which rose on the right of the road.

"I think," she went on, "you've never made that pilgrimage?"

"I have not. I have often meant to, but until now I have always put it off. I don't know why."

"Well, that is fortunate; but it is getting late; we must make haste, if you don't mind."

I turned my horse and we set off at a gallop.

As we rode along, I tried to account for this unexpected fancy which had an air of premeditation. I imagined that time and reflection had weakened the first impression that calumnies had made on Mlle. Marguerite. Apparently, she had conceived some doubts of Mlle. Hélouin's veracity, and had seized an opportunity to make, in an indirect way, a reparation which might be due to me. My mind full of such preoccupations, I gave little thought to the particular object of this strange ride. Still, I had often heard the tower of Elven described as one of the most interesting ruins of the country. I had never gone along either of the roads—from Rennes or from Josselin—which lead to the sea, without looking longingly at the confused mass rearing up suddenly among the distant heaths like some huge stone on end. But I had had neither time nor opportunity to examine it.

Slackening our pace, we passed through the village of Elven, which preserves to a remarkable extent the character of a mediæval hamlet. The form of the low, dark houses has not changed for five or six centuries. You think you are dreaming, when, looking into the big arched bays which serve as windows, you see the groups of mild-eyed women in sculpturesque costume plying their distaffs in the shade, and talking in low tones an unknown tongue. These gray spectral figures seem to have just left their tombs to repeat some scene of a bygone age, of which you are the only witness. It gives a sense of oppression. The sluggish life that stirs around you in the single street of the village has the same stamp of archaic strangeness transmitted from a vanished world.

A little way from Elven we took a cross-road that brought us to the top of a bare hillock. Thence, though still some distance off, we could plainly see the feudal colossus crowning a wooded height in front of us. The *lande* we were on sloped steeply to some marshy meadows inclosed by thickets.

We descended the farther side and soon entered the woods. Then we struck a narrow causeway, the rugged pavement of which must once have rung to the hoofs of mail-clad horses. For some time I had lost sight of the tower of Elven, and could not even guess where it was, when all at once it stood out like an apparition from among the foliage a few paces in front of us. The tower is not a ruin; it preserves its original height of more than a hundred feet, and the irregular courses of granite which make up its splendid octagonal mass give it the appearance of a huge block cut out but yesterday by some skilful chisel. It would be difficult to imagine anything more proud, sombre, and imposing than this old donjon, impassible to the course of ages, and lost in the depths of the forest. Full-grown trees have sprung up in the deep moats which surround it, and their tops scarcely touch the openings of the lowest windows. This gigantic vegetation, which entirely conceals the base of the edifice, completes its air of fantastic mystery. In this solitude, among these forests, before this mass of weird architecture, which seems to start up suddenly out of the earth, one thinks involuntarily of those enchanted castles in which beautiful princesses slept for centuries awaiting a deliverer.

"So far," said Mlle. Marguerite, to whom I had endeavoured to convey these impressions, "this is all I have seen of it, but if you want to wake the princess, we can go in. I believe there is always somewhere near a shepherd or shepherdess who has the key. Let us tie up the horses and search, you for the shepherd, and I for the shepherdess."

We put the horses into a small inclosure near and separated for a little while, but found neither shepherd nor shepherdess. Of course this increased our desire to visit the tower. Crossing a bridge over the moat, we found to our great surprise that the heavy door was not closed. We pushed it and entered a dark and narrow space choked with rubbish, which may have been the guard-room. We passed thence into a large, almost circular hall, where an escutcheon in the chimneypiece still displayed the bezants of a crusader. A large window faced us, divided by the symbolic cross clearly carved in stone. It lighted all the lower part of the room, leaving the vaulted and ruined ceiling in shadow. At the sound of our steps a flock of birds whirled off, sending the dust of ages on to our heads.

By standing on the granite benches, which ran like steps along the side of the walls, in the embrasure of the window, we could see the moat outside and the ruined parts of the fortress. But as we came in we had noticed a staircase cut out of the solid wall, and we were childishly eager to extend our discoveries. We began the ascent, I leading, and Mlle. Marguerite following bravely, and managing her long skirts as best she could. The view from the platform at the top is vast and exquisite. The soft hues of twilight tinged the ocean of half-golden autumnal foliage, the gloomy marshes, the fresh pastures, and the distant horizons of intersecting slopes, which mingled and succeeded each other in endless perspective. Gazing on this gracious landscape, in its infinite melancholy, the peace of solitude, the silence of evening, the poetry of ancient days fell like some potent spell upon our hearts and spirits. This hour of common contemplation and emotions of purest, deepest pleasure, no doubt the last I should spend with her, I entered into with an almost painful violence of enjoyment. I do not know what Marguerite was feeling; she had sat down on the ledge of the parapet, and was gazing into the distance in silence.

I cannot say how many moments passed in

this way. When the mists gathered in the lower meadows, and the distant landscape began to fade into the growing darkness, Marguerite rose.

"Come," she said in a low voice, as if the curtain had fallen on some beautiful spectacle; "come; it's over."

She began to descend the stairs, and I followed her.

But when we tried to get out of the donjon, to our great surprise we found the door closed. Most likely the doorkeeper, not knowing that we were there, had locked it while we were on the platform. At first this amused us. The tower was really an enchanted tower. I made some vigorous efforts to break the spell, but the huge bolt of the old lock was firmly fixed in its granite socket, and I had to give up all hope of moving it. I attacked the door itself, but the massive hinges and the oak panels studded with iron stolidly resisted all my efforts. Some stone mullions, which I found among the rubbish and hurled against the door, only shook the vault and brought some fragments from it to our feet. Mlle. Marguerite at last made me give up a task that was hopeless, and not without danger. I then ran to the window and shouted, but no one replied. For ten minutes I continued shouting, and to no purpose. We took advantage of the last rays of light to explore the interior of the donjon very carefully. But the door, which was as good as walled up for us, and the large window, thirty feet above the moat, were the only exits we could discover.

Meanwhile, night had fallen on the fields, and the shadows deepened in the old tower. The moonbeams shone in through the window, streaking the steps with oblique white lines. Mlle. Marguerite's gaiety had gradually died away, and she had even ceased to answer the more or less probable conjectures with which I still tried to calm her apprehensions. While she kept silent and immovable in the shadow, I sat in the full light on the step nearest the window, still shouting at intervals for help; but, to speak the truth, the more uncertain the success of my attempts became, the more I was conscious of a feeling of irresistible joyfulness. For suddenly I saw the eternal and impossible dream of lovers realized for me; I was shut in the heart of a desert and in the most complete solitude with the woman I loved. For long hours there would be but she and I in the world, but her life and mine. I thought of all the sweet evidences of protection and of tender respect it would be my right and my duty to show her. I imagined her fears at rest, her confidence restored, finally her slumbers guarded by me. I told myself, in rapture, that this auspicious night, though it could not give me her love, would at least insure me her unalterable respect.

As I yielded, with the egotism of passion, to my secret ecstasy, some trace of which, perhaps, expressed itself in my face, I was suddenly awakened by these words, spoken in a dull tone, and with affected calm:

"M. le Marquis de Champcey, have there been many cowards in your family before you?"

I rose, and immediately fell back again on the stone bench, looking stupidly into the darkness, where I saw dimly the ghostly figure of the young girl. Only one idea occurred to me—a terrible idea—that grief and fear had affected her reason—that she was going mad.

"Marguerite!" I cried, without knowing that I spoke.

The word no doubt put a climax to her irritation.

"My God, this is hateful!" she continued. "It is cowardly. I repeat, it is cowardly."

I began to see the truth. I descended one of the steps.

"What is the matter?" I said coldly.

She replied with abrupt vehemence: "You paid that man or child, whichever it was, to shut us up in this wretched tower. To-morrow I shall be ruined . . . my reputation lost . . . then I shall have perforce to belong to you. That was your calculation, wasn't it? But, I warn you, it will not serve you any better than the rest. You still know me very little if you think I would not prefer dishonour, the convent, death, anything, to the vileness of yielding my hand—my life—to yours. And suppose this infamous trick had succeeded, suppose I had been weak enough—which of a surety I never shall be—to yield myself, and what you covet more, my fortune to you, what kind of a man can you be? What mud are you made of, to desire wealth and a wife by such means? Ah! you may thank me for not yielding to your wishes. They are imprudent, believe me; for if ever shame and public ridicule drove me to your arms, I have such a contempt for you that I would break your heart. Yes, were it as hard and cold as these stones, I would press blood and tears from it!"

"Mademoiselle," I said, with all the calm I could command, "I beg you to return to yourself, to your senses. On my honour I assure you that you do me injustice. Think for a moment. Your suspicions are quite absurd. In no possible way could I have accomplished the treachery of which you accuse me; and even if I could have done so, when have I ever given you the right to think me capable of it?"

"Everything I know of you gives me this right!" she cried, lashing the air with her whip. "I will tell you once for all what has been in my thoughts for a long time. Why did you come into our house under a false name, in a false character? My mother and I were happy and at peace. You have brought trouble, anxiety, and sorrow upon us. To attain your object, to restore your fallen fortunes, you usurped our confidence . . . you destroyed our peace . . . you have played with our purest, deepest, and holiest feelings . . . you have bruised and shattered our hearts without pity. That is what you have done or tried to do, it doesn't matter which. Well, I am utterly weary of, utterly disgusted with, all this. I tell you plainly. And when now you offer to pledge your honour as a gentleman, the honour that has already allowed you to do so many unworthy things, certainly I have the right not to believe in it—I do not believe in it."

I lost all control of myself. I seized her

hands in a transport of violence which daunted her. "Marguerite, my poor child, listen. I love you, it is true, and a love more passionate, more disinterested, more holy, never possessed the heart of man. But you—you love me too! Unhappy girl, you love me and you are killing me. You talk of a bruised and a broken heart. What have you done to mine? But it is yours. I give it up to you. As for my honour, I keep it . . . it is intact, and before long I shall compel you to acknowledge this. And on that honour I swear that if I die, you will weep for me; that if I live—worshipped though you are—never, never, were you on your knees before me, would I marry you unless you were as poor as I, or I as rich as you. And now pray! pray! Ask God for a miracle; it is time!"

Then I pushed her roughly far from the embrasure, and sprang on to the highest step. A desperate idea had come to me. I carried it out with the precipitation of positive madness. As I have said, the tops of the beeches and oaks that grew in the moat were on the level of the window. With my bent whip I drew the ends of the nearest branches to me, seized them at random, and let myself drop into the void. I heard my name—"Maxime!"—uttered with a wild cry above my head. The branches I held bent their full length towards the abyss; there was an ominous crack, and they broke under my weight. I fell heavily on the ground. The muddy nature of the soil must have deadened the shock, for I felt that I was alive, though a good deal hurt. One of my arms had struck the stonework of the moat, and I was in such pain that I fainted. Marguerite's despairing voice recalled me to myself.

"Maxime! Maxime!" she cried, "for pity's sake, for God's sake, speak to me! Forgive me!"

I got up and saw her in the bay of the window, standing in an aureole of pale light, her head bare, her hair loose, her hands grasping the bar of the cross, while her glowing eyes searched the dark abyss.

"Don't be alarmed," I said; "I'm not hurt. Only be patient for an hour or two. Give me time to get to the château—that is the best place to go. You may be sure I shall keep your secret and save your honour, as I have just saved my own."

I scrambled painfully out of the moat and went to look for my horse. I used my handkerchief as a sling for my left arm, which was quite disabled and gave me great pain. The night was clear and I found the way easily. An hour later I was at the château. They told me that Dr. Desmarets was in the drawing-room. I hurried there and found him and a dozen others, all looking anxious and alarmed.

"Doctor," I said lightly as I came in, "my horse shied at his own shadow and came down in the road. I think my left arm is put out. Will you see?"

"Eh, what?—put out?" said M. Desmarets, after he had removed the handkerchief. "Your arm's broken, my poor boy."

Mme. Laroque started up with a little scream and came towards me.

"It seems we are to have an evening of misfortunes," she said.

"What else has happened?" I asked, as if surprised.

"I am afraid my daughter must have had an accident. She went out on horseback about three; it is now eight, and she has not returned!"

"Mlle. Marguerite? Why, I met her . . ."

"Met her? When? Where? Forgive a mother's selfishness, M. Odiot."

"Oh, I met her on the road, about five. She told me she thought of going as far as the tower of Elven."

"The tower of Elven! She has lost her way in the woods. We must send at once and search."

M. de Bévallan ordered horses to be got ready immediately. At first I pretended that I meant to be of the party, but Mme. Laroque and the doctor would not hear of it. Without much trouble I was persuaded to take to my bed, which, truth to tell, I needed badly. M. Desmarets attended to my arm, and then drove away with Mme. Laroque, who was to await the result of the search inaugurated by M. de Bévallan at the village of Elven.

About ten o'clock Alain came to tell me that Mlle. Marguerite had been found. He related the story of her imprisonment without omitting any details, except, of course, those known only to me and the young girl. The news was soon confirmed by the doctor, and afterwards by Mme. Laroque, and I had the satisfaction of seeing that no one suspected what had actually occurred.

I passed the night in repeating the dangerous leap from the window of the donjon with all the grotesque complications of fever and delirium. I did not get used to it. Every moment the sensation of falling through emptiness caught me by the throat, and I awoke breathless. At last day came, and I got calm. At eight o'clock Mlle. de

Porhoët came in and took her place at my bedside with her knitting in her hand. She did the honours of my room to the visitors who followed one another throughout the day. Mme. Laroque was the first after my old friend. As she held my hand and pressed it earnestly I saw tears on her face. Has her daughter confided in her?

Mlle. de Porhoët told me that old M. Laroque had been confined to his bed since yesterday. He had a slight attack of paralysis. To-day he cannot speak, and they are much alarmed about him. The marriage is to be hastened. M. Laubépin has been sent for from Paris; he is expected to-morrow, and the contract will be signed the following day, under his direction.

I have been able to sit up for some hours this evening, but, according to M. Desmarets, I should not have written while the fever was on me, and I am a great idiot.

October 3d.

Really it seems as if some malign power were hard at work devising the strangest and most cruel tests for my conscience and heart alternately.

M. Laubépin not having arrived this morning, Mme. Laroque has asked me to give her some of the information necessary for drawing up the general conditions of the contract, which is to be signed to-morrow. As I am obliged to keep my room for some days yet, I asked Mme. Laroque to send me the title-deeds and private documents in her father-in-law's possession, as they were indispensable for the clearing up of the points she had mentioned to me.

Very soon they brought me two or three drawers full of papers which they had taken out of M. Laroque's cabinet while he was asleep, for the old gentleman would never let any one touch his secret archives. On the first paper that I took up I saw my family name repeated several times. My curiosity was irresistibly aroused. Here is the literal text of the document:

To my Children

The name I bequeath to you, and which I have honoured, is not mine. My father's name was Savage. He was overseer of a large plantation in the Island of St. Lucia (then French), which belonged to a rich and noble family of Dauphiné—the Champcey d'Hauterives. In 1793 my father died, and, though I was quite young, I succeeded to the trust the Champceys reposed in him. Towards the end of that disastrous year the French Antilles were taken by the English or given up to them by the rebel colonists. The Marquis of Champcey d'Hauterive (Jacques-Auguste), whom the orders of the Convention had not yet struck down, then commanded the *Thetis* frigate, which had been cruising on this coast for three years. A good number of the French colonists of the Antilles had succeeded in realizing their fortunes, which had been in imminent peril. They had arranged with the Commandant de Champcey to get together a fleet of light transports, to which their property had been transferred, and which was to sail for France under the protection of the guns of the *Thetis*. In view of imminent disasters, I had myself received, a long time back, an order and authority to sell the plantation at any price. On the night of November 14, 1793, I put out alone in a boat for the Point of Morne-au-Sable and secretly left St. Lucia, already occupied by the enemy. I brought with me in English notes and guineas the amount I had received for the plantation. M. de Champcey, thanks to his intimate knowledge of the coast, had slipped past the English cruiser and had taken refuge in the dangerous and unknown channel of Gros-Ilet. He had instructed me to join him there this night, and only awaited my arrival to leave the channel with his convoy and make for France. In crossing, I fell into the hands of the English. These experts in treason gave me the choice of being shot on the spot or of selling them, for the million I had with me, which they agreed to leave in my hands, the secret of the channel where the fleet was hiding. I was young . . . the temptation was too great. Half an hour later the *Thetis* was sunk, the convoy taken, and M. de Champcey seriously wounded. A year passed—a year without sleep. . . . I was going mad. . . . I determined to make the cursed English pay for the remorse I suffered. I went to Guadeloupe; I changed my name; I devoted the larger part of the money I had received to the purchase of an armed brig, and I fell upon the English. For fifteen years I washed in their blood and my own the stain that in an hour of weakness I had brought on my country's flag. Though three parts of my fortune have been acquired in honourable combats, its origin was, nevertheless, the price of my treachery.

Returning to France in my old age, I ascertained the position of the Champcey d'Hauterives, and found that they were happy and wealthy. I kept my own counsel. I ask my children to forgive me. While I lived I had not the courage to blush before them. My death will reveal this secret to them. They must use it as their consciences may direct. For myself I have only one prayer to address to them. Soon or late there will be a final war between France and her neighbour. We hate one another too much; there's nothing else to be done; either we must devour them or they must devour us. If this war should be declared during the life of my children or grandchildren, I desire that they give to the state a corvette fully armed and completely equipped, on one condition, that it shall be called the *Savage*, and be commanded by a Breton. At each broadside she shall send on to the Carthaginian shore my bones will tremble with joy in my grave.

RICHARD SAVAGE, called LAROQUE.

The memories that this terrible confession awakened convinced me that it was correct. Twenty times I had heard my father relate with pride and indignation this incident in my ancestor's career. But in the family we believed that Richard Savage—I remember the name quite well—had been the victim, and not the contriver of the treason or mischance which had betrayed the commandant of the *Thetis*. Now I understand the peculiarities I had often noticed in the old sailor's character, and especially his thoughtful and timid bearing towards me. My father had always told me that I was the living portrait of my grandfather, the Marquis Jacques, and perhaps some dim perception of this resemblance had penetrated to the old man's troubled brain.

This revelation threw me into a terrible perplexity. I felt but little resentment against the unhappy man who had redeemed a moment of weakness by a long life of repentance, and by a passion of desperation and hatred which was not without greatness. Nor could I, without admiration, breathe the wild blast which animated the lines written by this guilty but heroic hand. Still, what was I to do with this terrible secret? My first thought was that it removed all obstacles between Marguerite and me; that henceforth the fortune that had kept us apart would be almost an obligatory bond, for I was the only person in the world who could regularize her title to it by sharing it with her. But in truth this secret did not belong to me, and though I had learned it by the purest of accidents, strict honesty, perhaps, demanded that I should leave it to come at its own time into the hands for which it was destined. But while I waited for that moment the irreparable would be accomplished. Eternal bonds were to be forged. The tomb was to close over my love, my hopes, and my sorrowful heart. And should I allow it when I might prevent it by a single word? And the day these poor women learned the truth, and blushed with shame to learn it, perhaps they would share my regret and despair. They would be the first to cry:

"Ah! if you knew, why did you not speak?"

No, neither to-day nor to-morrow, nor ever, shall those noble women blush for shame if I can prevent it. My happiness shall not be bought at the price of their humiliation. This secret is mine alone. The old man, henceforth speechless, cannot betray himself. The secret does not exist; the flames have destroyed it. I pondered it well. I know what I have dared to do. It was a will, a sacred document, and I have destroyed it. Moreover, it did not benefit me alone. My sister, who is intrusted to my care, might have found a fortune there, and, without consulting her, I have plunged her back into poverty. I know all that, but I will not allow two pure proud souls to be crushed and dishonoured by the burden of a crime of which they are ignorant. There is a principle of equity at stake far superior to mere literal justice. If, in my turn, I have committed a crime, I will answer for it. But the struggle has exhausted me. I can do no more now.

October 4th.

M. Laubépin, after all, arrived yesterday. He came to see me. He was brusque, preoccupied, and seemed ill-pleased. He spoke briefly of the marriage.

"A very satisfactory business!" he said; "in all respects an excellent combination, where nature and society both receive the guarantees they have the right to require in such matters. And so, young man, good-night. I have to smooth the delicate ground of the preliminary agreements, that the hymeneal car of this interesting union may reach its goal without jolting."

At one o'clock this afternoon the family assembled in the drawing-room with all the preparations and formalities observed at the signing of a marriage contract. I could not attend this ceremony, and I blessed my broken arm for sparing me the trial. About three I was writing to little Hélène, and taking care to assure her more strongly than ever of my complete devotion to her, when M. Laubépin and Mlle. de Porhoët came into my room. In his frequent visits to Laroque, M. Laubépin has learnt to appreciate my venerable friend, and the two old people have formed a respectful and Platonic attachment, which Dr. Desmarets tries in vain to misrepresent. After an exchange of ceremonies, of interminable bows and courtesies, they took the chairs I offered them, and both set about considering me with an air of grave beatitude.

"Well," I said, "it's over?"

"Yes," they replied in chorus, "it's over."

"It went off well?"

"Very well," said Mlle. de Porhoët.

"Wonderfully well," said M. Laubépin. After a pause he added: "Bévallan's gone to the devil!"

"And the young Hélouin after him!" continued Mlle. de Porhoët.

I exclaimed in surprise:

"Good God! what has happened?"

"My friend," said M. Laubépin, "the contemplated union had every possible advantage, and it would have without doubt insured the common happiness of both the parties concerned, if marriage were a purely commercial partnership; but it is nothing of the sort. As my assistance had been asked, I thought it my duty to bear in mind the inclination of the hearts and the agreement of the character just as much as the relative proportions of the estates. Now, from the first, I had the impression that the contemplated marriage had one drawback. It pleased no one, neither my excellent friend Mme. Laroque, nor the amiable *fiancée*, nor their most sensible friends—no one, in fact, except perhaps the *fiancé*, about whom I trouble myself very slightly. It is true (I quote here from Mlle. de Porhoët), it is true, I say, that the *fiancé* is *gentilhomme*. . . ."

"A *gentleman*, if you please," Mlle. de Porhoët interrupted severely.

"A *gentleman*," continued M. Laubépin, accepting the correction, "but it is a kind of *gentleman* I don't care for."

"Nor I," said Mlle. de Porhoët. "There are curious specimens of the kind. Dissipated stablemen, such as those whom we saw last century deserting their English stables under the direction of the Duc de Chartres to come over here and prepare the Revolution."

"Oh, if they had only prepared the Revolution," said M. Laubépin, sententiously, "we should forgive them."

"A million apologies, my dear sir; but—speak for yourself! Besides, that is not the question; will you go on?"

"So," continued M. Laubépin, "seeing that

every one was approaching this wedding as if it were a funeral, I searched for some honourable and legal means, not to break the engagement with M. de Bévallan, but to get him to withdraw voluntarily. This proceeding was the more justifiable, as in my absence M. de Bévallan had profited by the inexperience of my excellent friend, Mme. Laroque, and the weakness of my colleague in the neighbouring town, to make the most exorbitant demand in his own interests. Without departing from the wording of the agreements, I succeeded in materially altering their spirit. But there were limits which honour and the engagements already entered into forbade me to pass. And the contract remained favourable enough to be accepted with confidence by any high-minded man who had a sincere affection for his betrothed. Was M. de Bévallan such a man? We had to take that risk. I confess that I was not free from emotion when I began to read the irrevocable document before an imposing audience this morning."

"As for me," interrupted Mlle. de Porhoët, "I hadn't a drop of blood left in my veins. The first part of the contract conceded so much to the enemy that I thought all was lost."

"No doubt, mademoiselle; but, as we augurs

say among ourselves, 'the sting is in the tail,' *in cauda venenum.*

"It was comical, my friend, to see the faces of M. de Bévallan and my *confrère* from Rennes, who assisted him, when I suddenly unmasked my batteries. At first they looked at each other in silence; then they whispered together; at last they rose, and, coming to the table where I sat, asked me in a low voice for an explanation.

"'Speak up, gentlemen, if you please,' I said to them. 'We must have no mysteries here. What have you to say?'

"The company began to prick up their ears. Without raising his voice, M. de Bévallan suggested to me that the contract showed mistrust.

"'Mistrust, sir!' I replied, in my most impressive tone. 'What do you intend to convey by that? Do you make that strange imputation against Mme. Laroque, or against me, or against my *confrère* here present?'

"'S–s–sh! Silence! No wrangiing!' said the Rennes notary discreetly; 'But listen: it was agreed in the first place that the legal system of dotation should not be insisted on.'

"'The legal system? And where do you find that mentioned?'

" 'Oh, my dear sir, you know that you have practically reconstituted it by a subterfuge.'

" 'Subterfuge, monsieur? Allow me, as your senior, to advise you to withdraw that word from your vocabulary.'

" 'But, after all,' murmured M. de Bévallan, 'I'm tied hand and foot, and treated like a school-boy.'

" 'Indeed, sir! What, in your opinion, are we here for at this moment—a contract or a will? You forget that Mme. Laroque is living; that her father is living, and that it is a question of marriage, not of inheritance—at least, not yet. . . . Really, you must have a little patience; you must wait a little.'

" At these words Mlle. Marguerite rose.

" 'That is enough,' she said.—'M. Laubépin, throw that contract into the fire. Mother, let this gentleman's presents be returned.'

" Then she rose and left us like an outraged queen. Mme. Laroque followed her, and at the same time I threw the contract into the fireplace.

" 'Sir,' said M. de Bévallan in a threatening tone, 'there's some trickery in this, and I will find it out.'

" 'Sir,' I replied, 'allow me to explain it to you. A young lady, who, with a just pride, values herself very highly, feared that your offer might have been influenced by her wealth; she wished to be certain; she has no longer any doubts. I have the honour to wish you good-day!'

"Thereupon, my friend, I went after the ladies, and—upon my honour they embraced me.

"A quarter of an hour later, M. de Bévallan left the château with my colleague from Rennes. His departure and disgrace have naturally loosened the servants' tongues, and very soon his imprudent intrigue with Mlle. Hélouin was revealed. The young lady, already suspected on other grounds for some time past, has asked to be released from her duties, and the request has been granted. It is needless to say that our ladies will secure her future.

"Well, my dear fellow, what do you say to all this? Are you worse? You're as pale as death!"

This unexpected news had aroused so many emotions—pleasant and painful—that I felt myself on the point of losing consciousness.

M. Laubépin, who has to leave at daybreak to-morrow, came back this evening to wish me farewell. After some embarrassed remarks from us both, he said:

"Never mind, my dear boy, I'll not cross-examine you on what is going on here; but if you should require a confidant and a counsellor, I ask you to give me the preference."

As a matter of fact, I could not confide in a heart more sympathetic or more friendly. I gave the worthy old gentleman the particulars of my relations with Mlle. Marguerite. I even read some pages of this journal to him to show him more exactly the state of affairs, and also the state of my heart. I hid nothing from him save M. Laroque's secret.

When I had finished, M. Laubépin, who had suddenly become very thoughtful, began:

"It is useless to conceal from you, my friend, that when I sent you here I intended you to marry Mlle. Laroque. At first everything went as I wished. Your hearts, which I believe are worthy of one another, could not associate without sympathizing, but this strange event, of which the tower of Elven was the romantic scene, entirely disconcerts me, I must confess. Allow me to tell you, my young friend, that to jump out of window at the risk of breaking your neck was in itself a more than sufficient proof of your disinterestedness. It was quite superfluous to add to this honourable and considerate proceeding a solemn oath never to marry this poor girl except in contingencies we cannot possibly expect to see realized. I pride myself on being a man of resource—but I fully recognise that I cannot give you two hundred thousand francs, or take them away from Mlle. Laroque."

"Then tell me what to do, sir. I have more confidence in you than in myself, for I see that misfortune, which is always exposed to suspicion, has made me excessively susceptible on questions of honour. Speak. Do you counsel me to forget the imprudent but still solemn oath which alone at this moment separates me from the happiness you had imagined for your adopted son?"

M. Laubépin rose; his thick eyebrows drawn down over his eyes, he strode about the room for some minutes, then, stopping in front of me and seizing my hand, he said:

"Young man, it is true that I love you like my own child; but, even at the cost of breaking your heart and my own, I will not be false to my principles. It is better in matters of honour to do too much than too little, and as regards oaths, all those that are not extorted at the point of the knife or the mouth of a pistol, should either not be taken or should be kept. That is my opinion."

"It is mine too. I will leave with you to-morrow morning."

"No, Maxime, stay here a little longer. I do not believe in miracles, but I believe in God, who seldom allows us to be ruined by our virtues. Give Providence more time. I know that I am asking a very courageous effort from you, but I claim it formally from your friendship. If within a month you do not hear from me—well—then you can leave."

He embraced me and left me to my quiet conscience and my desolate heart.

October 12th.

It is now two days since I have been able to leave my retirement and appear at the château. I had not seen Mlle. Marguerite since we separated at the tower of Elven. She was alone in the *salon* when I entered. Recognising me, she made—involuntarily—an effort to rise. Then she sat motionless, and a flood of burning crimson dyed her face. It was infectious, for I felt that I was blushing to the forehead.

"How are you, M. Odiot?" she said, holding out her hand, and she spoke these simple words so gently, so humbly—alas! so tenderly too—that I longed to throw myself on my knees before her.

But I had to answer in a tone of icy politeness. She looked sadly at me, lowered her great eyes with an air of resignation, and went on with her work.

Almost at the same moment her mother called to her to come to her grandfather, whose condition had become most alarming. For some days now he had lost voice and movement; the paralysis was almost total. The last gleams of mental life were extinguished; only physical sensibility and the capacity for suffering remained. The end was not far off, but in this energetic heart life was too deeply rooted to be relinquished without an obstinate struggle. The doctor had foretold that his agony would last a long time. Still, at the first appearance of danger, Mme. Laroque and her daughter had tended him with the passionate self-sacrifice and utter devotion which are the special virtue and glory of their sex. The day before yesterday they broke down exhausted. M. Desmarets and I offered to take their places by M. Laroque to-night, and they agreed to have a few hours' rest. The doctor, who was very much fatigued, soon told me that he was going to throw himself on the bed in the next room.

"I am no use here," he said; "the thing is

over. You see the poor old fellow doesn't suffer any more. That lethargic state is not painful. The awakening will be death. So we can be quiet. Call me if you see any change, but I think it won't come till to-morrow. I'm dying for a sleep."

He gave a great yawn and went out. His language and his conduct before the dying man had shocked me. He is an excellent man; but to render to death the respect that is due to it, one must not see only the brute matter it dissolves, but believe in the immortal essence it releases.

Left alone in the chamber of death, I sat near the foot of the bed, where the curtains had been withdrawn, and I tried to read by a lamp that stood on a little table near me. The book slipped from my hands. I could think only of the strange combination of events which, after so many years, gave this guilty old man the grandson of his victim as witness and guardian of his last sleep. Then, in the tranquility of that hour and place, I recalled, in spite of myself, the scenes of tumult and bloody violence which had filled the life that was now ebbing away. I looked for traces of it on the face of the dying old man and on the large features defined in the shadow with the pale distinctness of a plaster mask. I saw only the solemnity and premature peace of the tomb. At intervals I went to the bedside to make sure that the weakened breast still heaved with vital breath. Towards the middle of the night an irresistible torpor seized me, and I slept, leaning my forehead on my hand. Suddenly I was awakened by a strange and sinister sound. I looked up, and a shudder ran through the marrow of my bones. The old man was half-sitting up in bed, staring at me with an intent, astonished look, and an expression of life and intelligence that I had not seen in him before. When our eyes met he started, stretched out his arms, and said, in a beseeching voice, whose strange unknown quality almost stopped the beating of my heart:

"Marquis, forgive me!"

In vain I tried to rise, to speak. I sat petrified in my chair.

After a silence, during which the dying man's eyes were still fixed on mine beseechingly, he repeated:

"Marquis, deign to forgive me."

At last I summoned up strength to go to him. As I approached he drew back fearfully, as if shrinking from a dreadful contact. I raised my hand, and lowering it gently before his staring and terror-stricken eyes:

"Rest in peace," I said; "I forgive you."

Before I had done speaking, his withered face lighted up with a flash of joy and youth. Two tears burst from his dry and sunken orbits. He stretched a hand to me, then suddenly the hand stiffened in a threatening gesture, and I saw his eyes roll between their dilated lids, as if a ball had gone through his heart.

"Oh, the English!" he whispered, and immediately fell back on the pillow like a log. He was dead. I called quickly, and the others came. Soon he was surrounded by pious mourners, weeping and praying for him. I retired, my soul deeply moved by this extraordinary scene, which I had resolved should ever remain a secret between myself and the dead man.

This sad event brought me cares and duties which I needed to justify me in my own eyes for remaining in the house. I cannot fathom M. Laubépin's motives for advising me to delay my departure. What did he hope from it? To me he seems to have yielded to a vague presentiment and childish weakness, to which a man of his stamp should never have given way, and to which I also was wrong to submit. Why did he not see that besides bringing additional suffering on me, he put me in a position that is neither manly nor dignified? What am I to do here now? Would they not have good reason to reproach me with trifling with sacred feelings? My first interview with Mlle. Marguerite had shown me how hard and how unbearable was the trial to which I had been condemned. The death of M. Laroque would make our relations easier, and give my presence a sort of propriety.

October 26th, Rennes.

All is over! God, how strong that tie was! How it held my heart, and how it has torn it as it broke! Yesterday evening about nine, as I leaned on my open window, I was surprised to see a faint light coming towards my house through the dark alleys of the park, and from a direction which the servants at the château do not frequent. A moment afterward there was a knock at my door and Mlle. de Porhoët came in breathless.

"Cousin," she said, "I have business with you."

I looked straight at her.

"A misfortune?" I said.

"No, it is not precisely that. Besides, you shall judge for yourself. My dear child, you have passed two or three evenings this week at the château. Have you noticed nothing unusual, nothing peculiar, in the attitude of the ladies?"

"Nothing."

"Have you not even noticed an unusual serenity in their appearance?"

"Perhaps I have. Allowing for the melancholy due to their recent sorrow, they seemed calmer and happier than before."

"No doubt. Other things would have struck you if, like me, you had lived in daily intimacy with them for fifteen years. Thus, I have observed signs of some secret understanding and mysterious agreement between them. Moreover, their habits have been largely altered. Mme. Laroque has given up her *braséro*, her sentry-box, and all her little Creole fancies. She rises at marvellous hours, and at daybreak instals herself with Marguerite at the work-table. They are both taken with a sudden passion for embroidery, and have ascertained how much a woman can earn at that work in a day. In short, there is a riddle to which I cannot find the answer. But it has been told me, and though I may be intruding on your secrets, I thought it right to inform you at once."

I assured Mlle. Porhoët of my absolute confidence in her, and she continued:

"Mme. Aubry came to see me this evening secretly. She began by throwing her wretched arms round my neck, which displeased me very much. Then, to the accompaniment of a thousand jeremiads about herself—which I will spare you—she begged me to stop her relations on the brink of ruin. This is what she has heard, through listening at doors, according to her pretty habit: The ladies are trying to get permission to transfer all their property to a community at Rennes, so as to do away with the difference of fortune which separates you and Marguerite. As they can't make you rich, they will make themselves poor. I thought it impossible to let you remain ignorant of this determination, which is equally worthy of those generous souls and of those Quixotic heads. You will forgive my adding that it is your duty to put an end to this design at any cost. I need not point out the regrets it will infallibly bring to our friends, nor the terrible responsibility it will throw on you. That you will see at a glance. If, my friend, you can from this moment accept the hand of Marguerite, everything will end in the best way possible. But in that respect you have tied yourself by an engagement which is not the less binding because it was made imprudently and blindly. There is then only one thing for you to do—to leave this country and resolutely extinguish all the hopes that your presence here must inevitably encourage. When you are no longer here I shall have less difficulty in bringing these two children to reason."

"Very well. I am ready. I will go this very night."

"Good!" she said. "When I give you this advice I obey a very rigorous law of honour. You have made the last moments of my long solitude pleasant, and you have given me back the illusion of the sweet attachments of life, which I had lost for so many years. In sending you away I make my last sacrifice; it is immense."

She rose and looked at me for a moment without speaking.

"At my age we do not embrace young people," she continued, smiling sadly; "we bless them. Adieu, dear child, and thank you. May God keep you!"

I kissed her trembling hands, and she left me hastily.

I hurriedly prepared for my departure, and then wrote a few lines to Mme. Laroque. I begged her to renounce a decision the effect of which she could not foresee, and which, for my part, I was determined to have no share in. I gave her my word—which she knew she could rely on—that I would never accept my happiness at the cost of her ruin. And I finished—for the sake of dissuading her from her fantastic project—by speaking vaguely of a future which might bring me fortune.

At midnight, when everything was silent, I said farewell, a bitter farewell, to the old tower where I had suffered—and loved—so much. I slipped into the château by a secret door of which I had the key. Furtively, like a criminal, I passed along the empty and resounding galleries, guiding myself as I best could in the dark. At last I reached the *salon* where I had first seen her. She and her mother had not long left it, and their recent presence was revealed by a sweet and pleasant perfume which transported me. I searched, and I touched the basket where a few moments before she had replaced her embroidery. Alas, my poor heart!

I fell on my knees before the seat she generally occupies, my forehead against the marble. I wept. I sobbed like a child. God, how I loved her!

The last hours of the night I spent in reaching

the little town secretly, and thence I drove to Rennes this morning.

To-morrow evening I shall be in Paris. O poverty, solitude, and despair, which I had left there, I shall find you again! Last dream of youth—dream of heaven, farewell!

PARIS.

The next day, in the morning, as I went to the railway station, a post-chaise stood in the courtyard of the hotel, and I saw old Alain get out. His face brightened as he saw me.

"Oh, sir, what good luck! You've not gone! Here is a letter for you."

I recognised M. Laubépin's writing. He said that Mlle. de Porhoët was seriously ill and was asking for me. I only allowed time to change the horses, and threw myself into the chaise, after forcing Alain to get in with me. I questioned him eagerly, and made him repeat his news, which seemed incredible.

The evening before, Mlle. de Porhoët had received an official despatch through M. Laubépin, announcing her succession to the entire Spanish property.

"And it seems," said Alain, "that she owes it to you, sir, for finding some old papers in the pigeon-house that have proved the old lady's title. I don't know how much truth there is in this, but if it is so, what a pity she has those ideas about the cathedral and won't give them up, for she's more bent on it than ever. When she first got the news she fell flat on the floor, and we thought she was dead. But an hour after she began talking about her cathedral, the choir, and the nave, the north aisle and the south, the chapter, and the canons. To calm her we had to fetch an architect and masons, and put the plans of her blessed building on her bed. At last, after three hours of that kind of talk, she quieted down a bit and dozed. When she awoke she asked for you, sir—M. le Marquis" (Alain bowed, closing his eyes)—"and I had to run after you. It seems she wants to consult you about the rood-loft."

This strange event took me entirely by surprise. Nevertheless, my memory, aided by the confused details given me by Alain, enabled me to find an explanation, which more precise information completely confirmed. As I have before said, the affair of the Spanish inheritance of the Porhoëts had gone through two phases. There had first been a long lawsuit between Mlle. de Porhoët and one of the great families of Castile, which my old friend had finally lost. Then there had been a new suit between the Spanish heirs and the Crown, the latter claiming on the grounds of intestacy.

Shortly after this, while pursuing my researches in the Porhoët archives, I had, about two months before leaving the château, laid hands upon a curious document, which I will here transcribe:

"Don Philip, by the Grace of God, King of Castile, Leon, Aragon, the two Sicilies, Jerusalem, Navarre, Grenada, Toledo, Valencia, Galicia, Majorca, Seville, Sardinia, Cordova, Cadiz, Murcia, Jaen, of the Algarves, of Algeciras, Gibraltar, the Canary Islands, the West and East Indies, the islands and continents of the ocean, the Archduchy of Austria; Duke of Burgundy, Brabant, and Milan; Count of Hapsburg, Flanders, the Tyrol, and Barcelona; Lord of Biscay and Molina, etc.

"To thee, Hervé-Jean Jocelyn, Lord of Porhoët-Gaël, Count of Torre Nuevas, etc., who hast followed me throughout my dominions, and served me with exemplary fidelity, I promise, by special favour, that in case of the extinction of thy direct and legitimate progeny, the possessions of thy house shall return, even to the detriment of my Crown, to the direct and legitimate descendants of the French branch of the Porhoët-Gaëls, as long as any such shall exist.

"And I make this covenant for myself and for my successors on my royal faith and word.

"Given at the Escorial, April 10, 1716.

"YO EL REY."

Together with this document, which was merely a translator's copy, I found the original text, bearing the arms of Spain. The importance of this document had not escaped me, but I had feared to exaggerate it. I greatly doubted whether the validity of a title of such ancient date, and prior to so many momentous events, would be recognised by the Spanish Government. I even doubted whether it would have the power to give effect to it, even if it had the will. I had therefore decided to say nothing to Mlle. de Porhoët about a discovery, the consequences of which seemed to me most problematic, and I had contented myself with sending the document to M. Laubépin. As I had heard nothing more of it, I had soon forgotten it in the midst of the personal cares with which I was overwhelmed at the time. However, contrary to my unjust suspicions, the Spanish Government had not hesitated to carry out Philip V's covenant, and at the very moment when a supreme decree had handed over the vast possessions of the Porhoëts to the Crown, it had nobly restored them to the legitimate heir.

About nine that evening I stopped at the humble house where this royal fortune had arrived so tardily. The little servant opened the door. She was crying.

From the staircase above came the grave voice of M. Laubépin.

"It is he," said the voice.

I went up the stairs quickly. The old man grasped my hand warmly, and took me into Mlle. de Porhoët's room. The doctor and the curé stood silent in the shadow of the window. Mme. Laroque knelt at the bedside; her daughter was arranging the pillow where the pale face of my old friend rested. When the sick woman saw me a faint smile flickered across her face. Painfully she moved one of her arms. I took her hand; I fell on my knees; I could not keep back my tears.

"My child," she said, "my dear child!"

Then she looked intently at M. Laubépin. The old notary took from the bed a piece of paper, and, as if he were continuing to read after an interruption, he went on:

"For these reasons," he read, "I appoint by this holograph will Maxime-Jacques-Marie Odiot, Marquis de Champcey d'Hauterive, noble by heart as by descent, sole and universal legatee of all my property in Spain as well as in France, without reserve or condition. Such is my will.

"JOCELYNDE JEANNE,

"COMTESSE DE PORHOËT-GAËL."

In my astonishment I had risen and was about to speak, when Mlle. de Porhoët, gently retaining my hand, placed it in Marguerite's. At this sudden contact the dear creature trembled. She bent her young forehead on the mournful pillow, and, blushing, whispered something in the dying woman's ear. I could not speak. I fell on my knees, and prayed to God. Some minutes passed in solemn silence, when Marguerite suddenly withdrew her hand with a gesture of alarm. The doctor came up hastily. I rose. Mlle. de Porhoët's head had fallen back; with a fixed and radiant glance she looked towards heaven; her lips half-opened, and as if she were speaking in a dream, she whispered:

"God! the good God! I see Him there . . . up there. . . . Yes . . . the choir . . . the golden lamps . . . the windows . . . the sun everywhere. . . . Two angels kneeling before the altar . . . in white robes . . . their wings move . . . God, they are alive!"

This cry died on her lips, which remained smiling. She closed her eyes as if she were going to sleep, and suddenly an air of immortal youth fell on her face, making it almost unrecognisable to us.

Such a death, after such a life, had lessons with which I desired to fill my soul. I begged to be left alone with the priest in the room. This pious vigil will not, I believe, be unavailing. From that face, irradiated with a glorious peace, where a supernatural light seemed to glow, more than one forgotten or questioned truth came home to me with irresistible force. Noble and holy friend, well I knew that the virtue of sacrifice was yours! Now I see that you have entered into your reward.

About two hours after midnight, yielding to fatigue, I longed to breathe the fresh air for a moment. I went down the dark staircase and into the garden, avoiding the *salon* on the ground floor, where I had seen a light. The night was profoundly dark. As I approached the arbour at the end of the little inclosure, I heard a faint sound, and at the same moment a shadowy form detached itself from the foliage. I felt a sudden rapture; my heart leaped, and I saw the heavens fill with stars.

"Marguerite!" I cried, holding out my arms. I heard a little cry, then my name murmured faintly, then silence . . . and I felt her lips on mine. I thought that my soul was escaping from me.

. . . .

I have given Hélène half my fortune. Marguerite is my wife. I close these pages forever. I have nothing more to intrust to them. What has been said of nations may be said of men: "Happy are those who have no history."

THE PORTRAITS OF OCTAVE FEUILLET

THE PORTRAITS OF OCTAVE FEUILLET

OCTAVE FEUILLET
In 1850.
After a drawing by the engraver Monciau.

In spite of the fashionable popularity achieved by Octave Feuillet as early as the year 1855, a popularity which never waned to his last hour, it seems that his life, which we should have pictured excessively brilliant and public, was in reality quiet and retired. The author of *M. de Camors* and of the *Roman d'un Jeune Homme Pauvre* was, as his portraits attest, melancholy of temperament and contemplative of mind, a man who was happiest in his own study, who preferred the distant echoes of his literary triumphs in his home, to noisy manifestations thereof in the world of social pleasure.

The Portraits of Octave Feuillet

Feuillet was the official novelist of the Second Empire, the pet writer of the *Revue des Deux Mondes.* He was received at Court among the distinguished guests who had the *entrée* at Compiègne and Fontainebleau. His plays and *proverbes* were acted in the Imperial theatres, at fashionable watering-places, and on the miniature stages of marionettes. The Empress treated him with marked distinction. It is difficult to understand why an author so honoured and so much sought after should have left so few portraits — canvases, medallions, water-colours, or engravings. Feuillet evidently was not lavish of his time in his sittings to artists, for neither Dubufe, nor Carolus-Duran, nor Winterhalter reproduced his features—a fact we find it almost hard to believe of a man who enjoyed the popularity of Feuillet. But we must accept the fact.

OCTAVE FEUILLET
In 1879.
After a sketch made in Geneva.

Mme. Octave Feuillet, to whom I went for final confirmation of this supposed dearth of artistic documents relating to her deceased hus-

OCTAVE FEUILLET.
After a photograph taken in 1880.

band, showed me everything she had as mementoes of the delicate psychologist to whose success she so largely contributed by her feminine diplomacy, her social observations, and her subtle and very cultivated mind.

"Alas!" she said, "I do not know why I am not richer in pictures of my dear lost one, for he had endless opportunities of being painted, but he was always too nervous and too busy to undertake the sittings proposed by various artists. This is why I can only show you a little portrait painted by Bonvin just before 1850, which represents him with a Musset-like face, and agrees pretty closely with a drawing of the same period by the en-

OCTAVE FEUILLET.
The last photograph taken in 1889.

graver Monciau, which could easily be reproduced."

"Beyond these souvenirs of Octave Feuillet as a young man," continued his widow, "I have

OCTAVE FEUILLET.
Sketch by Dantan, about 1878.

nothing but a drawing by Dantan, made at the time of the great success of the *Sphinx* at the Comédie Française, that is to say, about ten years before his death, and a large canvas by Hirch, a full-length, painted after 1880. But isn't it too dark for reproduction?"

To these portraits of the author of *Julia de*

Trécœur we may add a number of photographs, all of them taken after 1860. First, the large full-length portrait published by Goupil about 1869 in the *Galerie Contemporaine.* In spite of the defects inherent in all photographs, this is the most like him of all his portraits; it is reproduced as the frontispiece of this volume. We have given several others, among them one from Monciau's drawing, which shows us an Octave Feuillet of thirty-five, who is nevertheless somewhat morose-looking, and various presentments of the quinquagenarian Academician, with the white hair and gray beard of a man still in his prime, which offer a much nobler and more attractive semblance of the writer who has been called "The family Musset."

After the death of the famous novelist and playwright, the sculptor Crauck executed a fine bust of him with the aid of instructions given him by one of the author's sons, Richard Feuillet. Another bust, of little interest and a poor likeness, is at the Hôtel de Ville of St. Lo, where Feuillet was born, and where he often came to rest at his property during the summer.

Octave Feuillet's iconological record certainly does not arrest attention by any curious, startling, or hitherto unpublished elements. We have no childish or youthful portraits, nothing but the cold countenance of the man who had already "arrived"; no whimsical artistic sketch, not even any satirical caricature, to compromise, enliven, or give a Bohemian touch to the dignified attitude and severe correctness of the writer of the *Revue des Deux Mondes*. It is, we think, to be regretted. Octave Feuillet remains an over official-figure for us, bearing too obviously the stamp of the photographer's solemn poses, and sacramental "Quite still, please."

OCTAVE UZANNE.

THE END